A BRIDE FOR BRYNMOR

SONGBIRD JUNCTION

BOOK ONE

JACQUI NELSON

Cover design by Marlin

ISBN eBook: 978-0-9958596-7-8
ISBN Print: 978-1-7773113-0-8

PRAISE FOR THE SONGBIRD JUNCTION SERIES...

A Bride for Brynmor
Songbird Junction, Colorado - January 1877

"A special journey that kept me following along to see what would happen. I cannot wait to read about the other two sisters and also Brynmor's brothers turn out!" ~ Lori D.

"A perfectly written love story." ~ SKM

"Oh, I love this book. There is something about getting lost for a few hours in this era. So well written and descriptive, you feel like you are right there in all the action." ~ B

"A great love story with perilous danger." ~ Dorothy R.

A Bride for Heddwyn
Songbird Junction, Colorado - January 1877

"A splendid cast of characters...a book that will be re-read over and over again." ~ Crystal Crossings

I loved this couple. Heddwyn is perfect for Oriole and she for him." ~ Cheryl P.

"Throw in a cute puppy, a troop of gypsies, & meddling family, and the charming adventure is complete" ~ Michelle R.

"Mayhem, both funny and heart warming." ~ Betty R.

DEDICATION

For Liette Bougie, who has enriched my days in more ways
than I can express my gratitude for.

Thank you for sharing the delightful but also sometimes
daunting adventure of both storytelling and life.

CHAPTER 1

January 1878
Denver, Colorado

*A*lone in the shadows of the alley, Lark surveyed the sunny street filled with city folk who might end her family's escape if they— She shook her head, rejecting her doubt. *If* wasn't acceptable. She couldn't fail her sisters again.

Oriole and Wren *had* to make it to their pre-arranged meeting place across the street.

She tucked her nose under her scarf, thrust her hands deeper into her skirt pockets, and rocked on her boots. Nothing helped. Her shivers grew because they weren't from the frosty air or the snow-covered ground.

She trembled with dread that her pursuit of freedom might end in her sisters' deaths.

Oriole, sweet as she was savvy, had chosen this location. But two years earlier, when Oriole's violin required repairs, Oriole had been the only one allowed to enter Mrs. Fitzpatrick's Music Emporium.

Lark had been disappointed not to view the treasures inside. Today, she cared only for what she might see outside —her sisters, who'd agreed to meet at the music shop if they were separated fleeing Cheyenne. After sixteen years together, the last twelve days apart made her heart ache unbearably.

She kept searching for Wren's tiny and timid form—so easily lost in a crowd. And smothered there as well. Being a head shorter and a couple of years younger than Lark and Oriole hadn't helped Wren's confidence.

Wren may be the best singer in their three-woman songbird troupe, but she only shone when she performed in the circle of their act. She would suffer the most on her own.

How could she have lost them? She'd lied and schemed and surrendered everything to keep their trio together, including her liberty and the man she loved. How had it all gone so wrong?

Because Beelzebub wouldn't let his pawns go without a fight.

Their troupe manager, Ulysses T. Stone, was both a devil and a dog. He had a hound's nose for finding people he could bamboozle into giving him what he craved most: fortune and fame. He coveted an audience's attention as much as their money.

Anger stirred the turmoil in her heart. He may be the maestro of manipulation, but she was the granddaughter of Cree warriors. She would not fail Oriole and Wren. She would find them and take them far away from the man who'd vowed to never let them go.

She scanned the street for the wiry, dark-haired Irishman whose fake gentleman's accent and dandified clothing concealed a thug carrying an arsenal of weapons, including a spring-loaded derringer under one ruffled sleeve. No one, in disguise or plain sight, matched his stature.

She saw no sign of Oriole or Wren either. They'd agreed to meet at noon. Her pocket watch read five past one.

Accept it. There's no when *or* if. *They aren't coming.*

Or maybe they'd arrived earlier and gone? But not before leaving a message saying where. They'd agreed to do that as well.

Abandoning her hiding spot, she crossed the street at a brisk pace. The snow crunching under her feet marked her progress as she slipped into the alley flanking the music shop and examined the wall from top to bottom. When she rounded the back of the building, she found that alley empty as well. A stroke of luck.

She continued hunting for a crevice that held a piece of paper. There had to be a letter. Had she missed it? If she did a second pass, maybe she'd—

"Looking for something?" The words cracked like a whip, close behind her.

Cringing from the memory of his lash on her back, she spun to face Ulysses. The footlong strip of rawhide tied to his wrist remained lowered. A weapon she now feared had permanently scarred the one good Samaritan who'd been brave—and foolhardy—enough to step between her and her troupe manager.

"You won't find anything." Ulysses' smirk raised her hackles. "But I've found you. And with you in my grasp, your sisters will fall like dominoes back in line."

Despicable lout. He loved to boast how he could control everyone, including men twice his size. He was a master of skullduggery and savagery.

Lark had taken many of the punishments he meant for her sisters, but he'd always stopped short of striking her in the face or hands. If she couldn't sing or play an instrument, she couldn't earn him money. But when he'd seized her by the throat and squeezed so hard he'd hurt her vocal cords and made her voice raspy for days, Oriole and Wren had been adamant. They were finally leaving him.

He caught her arm and dragged her toward the street.

She forced herself not to struggle, to let him think he'd won, until they reached the thoroughfare and its people. Then she screamed. As loud as she could. "Fire! There's a fire in the music shop."

The crowd surged toward her and swept her free of Ulysses' hold. Unfortunately, they also hemmed her in. She braced her spine against the shop's clapboard front, surrounded, with nowhere to run.

"Where is it?" demanded a thin man with a wealth of wild hair. He swayed like a windswept scarecrow, trying to peer over the ring of bonnets, bowlers, and fur hats surrounding him. "I can't see no fire."

"Because there isn't one," a tight-lipped matron said as she adjusted her grip on her parcels. "There's nothing here."

I'm here. She scanned the crowd for a kind face.

When Wild Hair's eyes met hers, he went still as a sturdy oak. "What mischief are ya up to?"

The matron's gaze jumped from her packages to Lark. "Yes, making a false claim is a serious matter."

So is escaping Ulysses.

Who, with a glare so hot it could blister a frying pan, shoved through the crowd and reached for her again. "She's not right in her head. I'll take care of—"

She struck the inside of his elbow as she darted sideways. A maneuver she'd learned from watching him fight.

His pale skin turned a mottled red as he cursed and flicked his hand, trying to shake the tingling from the nerve she'd hit. She hadn't much time before he launched a strike she couldn't counter.

"It's a crime!" she proclaimed. "That's what it is."

Wild Hair leaned toward her, eager to hear more. "What is?"

"To lie about a fire. Take me to your sheriff," she added before Ulysses could object. "He'll reward you for removing me from your streets."

The townsfolk's odds of receiving compensation were better than hers for receiving fair treatment from the law. Mixed-blood women who'd grown up in orphanages had to forge their own paths. Her deliverance might occur on the way to the sheriff when her escorts relaxed their guard. She'd find an opening to escape them and Ulysses.

His expression had gone blank, which meant he was pondering something ugly. Maybe cracking his whip across her shoulder or hip, where the welt wouldn't show. If it weren't for their witnesses, he wouldn't have held back.

"I'll take her where she needs to go." For every stride he came closer, she took one back.

Until she ran out of room. Her gaze darted to his whip. She found his hand balled into a fist. Her stomach seized in anticipation of the worst. If she didn't dodge him again, she wouldn't be able to breathe or utter a word in her defense.

A smile twitched his lips. "Ladies and gentlemen, this madwoman's laborious little show is over. Don't waste any more time on her. Go home."

"Doing the right thing is never a waste," a divinely deep and familiar voice declared from the back of the crowd. "I'll go wherever she goes."

The sight of an auburn-haired giant clad in a fine wool

cap and a work-worn sheepskin coat trying not to topple her audience as he nudged them aside to reach her, filled her with delight and disbelief.

How had Brynmor Llewellyn known she was here? At this hour, he should be hauling freight with his brothers, not visiting this shop or his living quarters above it. A complication neither she nor her sisters had known about when they'd agreed to meet here.

The big Welshman only halted when he stood between her and Ulysses, shielding her, but also making it impossible for her to see around him and help him.

When she moved to stand by his side, he heaved a sigh. Another familiar sound. Comforting and troublesome. Why couldn't he understand? She didn't want him to take a blow that was meant for her.

"She shouldn't have begged you to interfere again." The return of Ulysses' bland expression as he stared at Brynmor made her shiver.

Brynmor snorted. "You don't know her very well. She's never asked me for anything."

Ulysses raised one brow mockingly. "And still you are here."

Brynmor's voice rumbled like a storm on the horizon. "And you were promising to take her where she needs to go, which is to the sheriff so he can hear what you've done."

"I've done my duty." Without taking his gaze off Brynmor, Ulysses angled his head to project his voice, loud and clear, to the crowd. "The law will agree. It's my responsibility and my *burden*"—he pressed his palm to his heart—"to be the guardian of this chit who, unfortunately, is both mentally disturbed and my niece."

"You're a caretaker," Brynmor growled, "who only cares for himself."

The care this usually soft-spoken giant had shown for his family and hers had been her undoing. When she'd first seen him in Cheyenne, she'd acted no different from anyone else. She'd admired his strength but found his size intimidating.

She'd kept him, and everyone else, at a distance.

Then she'd caught Wren following his sister in order to learn how a woman was doing a man's job. And Brynmor had caught her trying to persuade Wren to stay far away from the Llewellyn family.

He'd teasingly asked why Wren was spying on his sister. When Wren had cowered behind Lark and not said a word, he demanded to know if they needed his help. He'd been as concerned for strangers as he'd been for his own sister.

He'd told her, "No matter how challenging, family is a gift. So are good friends."

She stifled her own sigh. Back then, he hadn't met her *uncle* Ulysses and knew next to nothing about her. He'd always been generous with his viewpoint.

She wasn't a gift or a good friend or even a good person. She kept making things worse for everyone, while Brynmor did the opposite. He and his brothers were the reason their sister, Robyn, was so resiliently capable. After their parents died, all three brothers helped raise her. But Brynmor, as the eldest, had set the tone.

That voice...gentle but firm, playful but concerned had, for the first time in her life, made her feel safe. Her determination to keep him at a distance had wavered. He'd suffered deeply because of her weakness.

"Don't be fooled by this do-gooder's bungling of the facts." Ulysses yanked a wad of papers from his coat pocket and waved it in the air for everyone to see. "Look at the debts this woman has accumulated. Who will pay them if I don't? I'm bound to her by all of her liabilities, including her bastard, heathen blood."

When the crowd gasped, Ulysses' tone turned as grave as a vaudeville actor. "'Tis true. My brother fathered children out of wedlock with"—he sucked in a breath as if it caused him physical pain to say the next words—"*three Indian women*. But the hand of God intervened. He died, and his children were placed in a mission whose saintly Reverend Mother eventually found me. Their last family left on Earth. With too many to feed and house, she begged me to take my nieces."

An old lie with some truths. They all had Irish fathers who, instead of marrying their Cree mothers, had abandoned them. And after their mothers died, they ended up in the mission's orphanage.

But none of them were related.

She called Oriole and Wren her sisters because they were bound by love. Ulysses called them his nieces to keep them shackled to him and their work. How he'd found them at the church mission in the Qu'Appelle Valley, far to the north of here, had become a tangle of lies peppered with just enough truths to keep them under his power.

The charlatan ran his fingertips over the white streaking the temples of his otherwise pitch-black hair, calling attention to his wise old uncle persona. "The mission agreed that we should sign a contract of expectations. My nieces promised they would work to offset the cost of their upkeep."

"We never signed anything. You for—"

"Oh, unhappy deceiver!" He stabbed his finger at her for emphasis. "Since becoming unbalanced like her father, she will lie that her signature was forged."

Curse him! And her for hoping she might fight him with

words. While he had no musical talent, he had a flair for speeches and fabricating letters. Luckily, his abilities hadn't extended to learning Cree. If Oriole or Wren left a message, it would be written in that language, and only they could read it.

"She has paid any debt to you a thousand times over."

Brynmor's conviction made her stand taller. Every time she'd challenged Ulysses' lies, everyone else believed him and not her.

Ulysses thrust his papers higher. "These documents say otherwise."

"Do they also say you can own someone forever?" she muttered.

"He's a vile excuse for a human being." Brynmor's voice shook with fury. So did his entire body.

Astonishment froze her like a block of ice. She'd rarely seen him angry. And never like this, never on the precipice of losing control.

He leaned toward Ulysses, his hands fisted, ready to throw his own punch. "His actions are immoral and illegal."

"They most certainly are not. I have the legitimate right to—" The screech of the shop door opening behind Lark cut him off. He shoved his way, none too gently, through the crowd and back onto the street. "If you insist, I'll fetch the sheriff."

Another lie. He'd bring hired thugs before he involved the law. Unless... Had he, like he'd done in Cheyenne, already found a way to coerce Denver's lawmen into doing his bidding?

"When you find *whomever* you're going after, come to my freight office," Brynmor called after him. "We need to settle our own debt." The tension in him eased with each word he said, or maybe every stride Ulysses took away from them.

She allowed herself to relax as well. Brynmor hadn't known Ulysses as long as she had, but he understood him well enough. Standing with him like comrades in arms or, even better, like her heart's companion, made her smile. Until she focused on his final word. "What *debt* are you talking about?"

"I haven't repaid him for..." He shrugged as he gestured to the side of his face angled away from her.

She didn't need a direct sightline to know what was there. He referred to his clouded white eye.

The last of her euphoria fell to horror. Twelve days ago in Noelle, when she'd first heard about his injury, she'd suspected Ulysses' involvement. But she hadn't the strength to accept it. "Why didn't you listen to me in Cheyenne when I told you to never come near me again?"

He grimaced like she'd asked the unimaginable. "Because you needed help."

Damn your kindness. And my stupidity. If her pointing a rifle at him hadn't dissuaded him, why had she hoped her words would?

"And I did listen." He whispered his next words in her ear, so low and fast that only she could hear. "I left you, and my feet led me to Ulysses. He struck my eye with his whip and vowed no doctor in Cheyenne would treat my wound. He'd make sure of it. That's when I left you for good. My family dragged me to the next town. We kept wandering until we finally found Denver." He raised his head and faced the crowd. "Show's over," he told them. "For real this time. Nothing left to see or hear."

"Faith and begorrah, what did I miss?" a biting voice demanded from behind them. A woman with piercing jade eyes and a cloud of white hair piled high on her head stood in the doorway. "If I hadn't been in the middle of sealing a wicked crack on a mandolin, I would've shown my face sooner."

"Thank you," Brynmor said, "for arriving when you could, Mrs. Fitzpatrick."

The shop owner shook a finger as bent as her spine was straight. "Brynmor Llewellyn, you'd best answer my question." Her toe joined the rhythm of her still-admonishing finger, tapping the floorboards with a rising tempo.

Brynmor gestured to Lark. "My friend was being harassed by her troupe manager."

"My ex-manager." She raised her chin. "I no longer sing for him."

The woman's eyes narrowed as she evaluated Lark. "You're a songbird?"

"A talented one." The admiration in Brynmor's voice made her twitchy. "Lark is a gifted musician as well."

She shook her head. "That's all in the past." She wanted to be more than her voice. She wanted to be a good sister and friend. She wanted to be worthy of their faith in her.

Mrs. Fitzpatrick scowled in the direction Ulysses had disappeared. "But that loudmouth who departed so abruptly doesn't agree? What is his name?"

"Ulysses T. Stone," Brynmor replied.

"Some call him Tombstone," Lark added. "Because he enjoys bragging that he could put you under one."

"Charming," the shopkeeper muttered in a scornful tone. "I've never heard of him, but his type is all too common. And you, Miss...Lark? What is your family name?"

"I have none. My mother—" She clenched her teeth, regretting even that small a revelation. "My past is complicated."

"But not uncommon. A few years ago, I met a young lady who, like you, said she only had a first name and an unusual one too. I wish I'd—" She raised her gnarled hand as if to stop herself and whatever questions she probably sensed rising in Lark. "That's in the past as well."

Lark tensed with disbelief and apprehension. As a shop-keeper, Mrs. Fitzpatrick must have met hundreds of people. Was it Oriole she remembered most, or her violin?

"See to your future." The woman's demeanor held the enviable firmness of someone used to commanding her own destiny.

Was that how she managed to repair instruments with finesse using hands ravaged by swollen joints? Unrelenting determination?

"If that ruffian pesters you again, do not hesitate to seek refuge in my shop."

"No. You don't want him coming near you." Her gaze leapt from the shop owner to Brynmor. "You shouldn't either." She backed away from them. "I must leave." *And take my problems with me.*

Brynmor reached out to stop her, then just as quickly shoved his hands into his coat pockets. The boyish action pulled the tan leather tight across his manly shoulders. "There's no rush, is there?" His sigh sounded wistful. "Can't you spare a moment to stand with me and catch your breath?"

Wouldn't that be divine? Temptation halted her feet.

"You'd be wise to stay." Mrs. Fitzpatrick shrugged. "But in my experience, young folk hardly ever are. So, my dearie, I shall wish you Godspeed on your journey. And you, my boyo,"—she shook her finger at Brynmor again—"if I don't see you in my shop in a few minutes, I shall expect you this evening with a full account of your day's activities. Other-wise, I shall toss you from your lodgings." She closed the door behind her with a spirited snap.

Lark felt her jaw drop. "How much trouble have I caused you now?"

"None." Brynmor's chuckle soothed her more than his words. "Mrs. Fitzpatrick is my landlady and a friend. You can trust her."

She could also trust Ulysses to hurt the woman if he suspected they were friendly. "What if he comes back here?"

"He'll make it easier for me to find him."

She didn't like that prospect either.

"Why didn't you stay in Noelle?" he asked. "Why did *you* come back here?"

"For Oriole and Wren."

"They were here?" He spun in search of them.

She grabbed his arm to halt him and his worry. He went dead still, except for his breathing, which ratcheted up a notch as he stared at her hand on him.

She released him quickly. "We agreed to meet at noon, but I haven't seen them. Luckily, Ulysses hasn't either. How did you know I was here?"

"My sister sent a telegram."

"I should've guessed." She'd spent the last ten days in Noelle with Robyn and her new husband's family, the Peregrines, waiting for today. Now she knew why she'd boarded the train without any interference. Robyn had chosen to let her go, so Brynmor could deal with her. That showed how much his sister had transformed. After Cheyenne, all three of Brynmor's siblings had done everything they could to keep Lark away from him.

The change was another complication for her. And Brynmor too.

When he crossed his arms, the strength of his body and soul held her gaze captive. "You should've stayed in Noelle where more people are willing to protect you."

And who will protect them? And Mrs. Fitzpatrick, if she gets involved now as well?

She chose to stare at the music shop instead of him. "Safety in numbers is an illusion." *But being alone is worse.* "I must find my sisters, but first I need to leave a warning that Ulysses was here and—"

A terrible realization stole her voice. Ulysses now knew to look for letters hidden outside this shop! That complication left her muttering in frustration.

"I'm sure Mrs. Fitzpatrick would agree to give a message to your sisters whenever they arrive." Brynmor opened the shop door and held it wide, waiting for her to enter.

She hesitated. Brynmor may trust the woman, but Oriole said not to. But then again, Oriole questioned everyone's motives when they showed even the tiniest interest in her. She was sweet and savvy *and suspicious.* She'd said Mrs. Fitzpatrick had quizzed her about her violin and then offered an extraordinary sum for it—when the only thing remarkable about the instrument was how long Oriole had owned it.

"Come in," Mrs. Fitzpatrick ordered. "Before you let in all the cold air."

The shop owner's command nudged Lark to the door. The instruments on display drew her inside.

Rows of fiddles, banjos, mandolins, several pianos, even a few accordions and— She gasped with amazement. Mrs. Fitzpatrick had a hurdy-gurdy?

The rare find yanked her forward like a lasso 'round her heart. She'd had the exquisite pleasure of playing a gurdy for a year before she'd been forced to let it go.

She halted short of touching its intricate keybox. She couldn't buy it or keep it, so why covet it? Everything she had must go toward securing food and shelter for her sisters. And transportation. As far away from Ulysses as possible, which meant away from Brynmor as well.

Soon. But not right now. Her finger skimmed the taut drone strings then the polished wood, imagining she was once again touching Brynmor's arm as they danced.

"I hoped it might still interest you."

Her hand halted. "Still?"

"That everything you said in Cheyenne wasn't a fabrication."

She'd lied to him twice. First, about her hurdy-gurdy. Second when she said she wanted him to leave and never come near her again. "It's difficult to lie about everything. When you were in Cheyenne…" *It felt like a dream come true. Until it became a nightmare.*

She turned her back on the temptation he and the gurdy presented and went to the counter where Mrs. Fitzpatrick continued repairing the mandolin she'd mentioned earlier. Wren would've been drawn to the instrument as strongly as Lark had been to the hurdy-gurdy. Or Oriole to her violin. They all had their weaknesses.

"Mrs. Fitzpatrick…" She tried to keep her voice nonchalant, as if her hopes didn't hang on the woman's answer. "Has anyone visited your shop and left a message for, or asked for one from, a Miss Colm?"

"Whose name is that?"

"It was my father's." She sealed her lips against sharing anything more on that subject. Heaven help her if she said the truth. *My father only told my mother his first name.*

The shop owner set down her repair tools and gave Lark her full attention. "You told me you didn't have a last name."

"Colm is a name I only use for leaving messages for my sisters." Oriole had insisted they do this so Ulysses would have a harder time tracking them. They'd learned early in life that most people couldn't remember or repeat Cree names. The Llewellyn brothers' uncommon but still pronounceable names had become the inspiration for using the Irish names.

Mrs. Fitzpatrick stared at her as if she'd gone as batty as Ulysses had proclaimed on the porch outside.

Brynmor cleared his throat, then waited until the shop owner's glittering green eyes fixed on him. "Have you heard the name Colm recently?"

"No," the woman snapped.

"I'm sorry."

Mrs. Fitzgerald flinched as if Lark's apology rattled her more than the name. "Why?"

"I've upset you."

"My complaint is with the past, not you. Certain Irish names are too similar. They remind me of things I'm determined to forget." Mrs. Fitzpatrick's voice had resumed its brisk confidence, but her revelation made Lark pause.

None of this boded well for sharing her sisters' Irish names. They were *very* similar to Colm. But first came the letter, then the names. "May I leave a letter with you for my sisters who may come looking for a Miss Colm?"

"Yes, but if they also have *secret* names,"—she huffed as she shook her head over the possibility—"you'd best write *all* of your names on your letter so I don't forget."

Lark suspected the woman had never forgotten anything in her life. She pulled her notebook and pencil from her pocket and, in plain view of the shop owner, wrote:

Ȧ"Ȧ

"I shudder to ask," Mrs. Fitzpatrick said as she frowned

at the foreign letters, "but have you invented a language as well?"

Lark shook her head. "These symbols may not be well known, but they're no secret." She kept writing in the script used by her mother's people who lived north of the border in Canada.

Despite the missionaries wanting her and her sisters to learn only the colonial languages—to better assimilate them into the white world—Lark had taught Oriole and Wren to write in Cree. Their heritage was the second thing they'd bonded over in the orphanage. The first had been none of them speaking French in a community where most of the Métis and the missionaries shared that ancestry.

When she'd finished writing, her letter read:

ᐃᐦᐃ
ᓇᑕᐃ· ᓂᐣᒋ·ᐺᐊᐧᐟ. ᐊᔪᒋ ᒥᐦᗅ. ᑐᐣᒋᐸᕖ.
ᐃ·ᒃᐃᐤ. ᐅᓗᕒᒃᐃᐧᐤ. ᐊᐣᒉᐊ·ᑭᒥᐧ
ᐊᐦᐳ ᓇᑕᐃ ᐱᐦᐱᐦᕆᐤ. ᐁᑲ·. ᐅᓗᕒᒃᐃᐤ
ᐺᔰᐦᐁᐊᐧᒪᐧ ᐆᐷᘅˣ ᓀᐸᕒᒥᐦᐊᐃᐧᐤ
ᐱᐣᐅᐊᐧᕆᐊᐧᕒᐣ

Which translated to:

Enemy in sight!
Go to three brothers with red hair inhabiting Falcons'
storehouse
Or to Robin and Falcon family in the town noel
Meadowlark

She folded the paper and wrote on the outside:

For Miss Cillian and Miss Cavan.
From Miss Colm.

When she handed it to Mrs. Fitzpatrick, the woman's face turned white as birch bark. Lark instinctively stepped back.

"*You,*" the woman said in a strangled voice, "have a sister who knew someone named Cavan? That's as rare as Colm."

It was strange that all three of their mothers had known their father's first name but hardly anything else. Lark lied about many things, but she didn't appreciate being called a liar for something that, although fantastical, was true.

"The girl with the unusual eyes and the violin." Mrs. Fitzpatrick's hand shot over the counter, and the much too small space Lark had put between them, and seized Lark's wrist. "Where is she?"

She braced herself to break free. When her captor grabbed Brynmor's arm as well, she froze in shock.

Mrs. Fitzpatrick did not. She yanked them both closer to her. "Brynmor, you must take good care of this young lady and bring her sister back to me."

"Where they go is their decision. Not mine or yours." He spoke in a soothing tone, as if he were trying to calm a pair of spooked horses, one who might trample him and the other ready to bolt.

She yanked free of Mrs. Fitzgerald's shackle. The tidy shop filled with her favorite things bore down on her like a trap. Brynmor's footsteps shadowed hers. A slow, steady beat. He didn't chase. He simply followed.

Outside, she spun to face him as he paused to close the door. "I'll never bring Oriole back here! And nothing that woman does or says will ever change my mind." She rubbed her wrist, glaring at the faint red mark that enraged more than it hurt.

"She had a son named Cavan."

Had? Her anger departed as fast as it had arrived. "I didn't know. Neither did Oriole."

Or had she? Why had Oriole really suggested they meet at this shop and not somewhere else?

"No." She paced in a circle as she chanted the word in rising incredulity. "No. No. No! Did Mrs. Fitzpatrick's son play the violin?"

"Not well, according to her. She said that's why he had to pursue the fur trade and never returned."

She lurched to a halt. The history of the Qu'Appelle Valley had been heavily shaped by French trappers and their legacy, but they weren't the only ones. There'd been some Scottish and Irish fortune seekers as well.

"So..." Brynmor exhaled resignedly as he frowned at the shop. "It's not just her. You believe Oriole could be her granddaughter."

He'd never pried into their past, but he'd paid attention to what he saw and heard. Oriole had always been the girl with the violin. She'd been clutching it and Wren's hand when Lark had been dragged, kicking and screaming, into the orphanage.

If not for the two of them, she wouldn't have stopped. Or rather, switched. She'd started fighting for them.

"Oriole may no longer be an orphan." Envy pinched her heart, followed quickly by apprehension. She'd worried about her sisters for so long that she couldn't stop. What she wanted most for them was freedom. And Mrs. Fitzpatrick had swiftly gone from outspoken but helpful to aggressively controlling.

A long silence stretched between her and Brynmor before he asked, "What are you planning to do?"

"I'll keep hunting for my sisters." She'd figure out the rest later.

"Here or in Cheyenne?"

"They wouldn't go back there. Too many in Cheyenne owe Ulysses a debt. He'll have his spies watching for us." She leaned against a porch pillar as she contemplated the street ahead of her.

She hadn't gotten far since she'd given up her hiding spot on the other side. Her journey from Cheyenne to Denver had been costly. Getting her sisters even farther before secreting them away in a new home would drain her savings.

She pushed away from her post with a purpose. "I need to find work."

"I know a man who'd like to hire someone to help with a shipment to Noelle."

"You mean you?" She scoffed in disbelief. "You're too good at your job to require assistance."

"This cargo is different." He spread his hands wide as if the disparity was huge.

"It's dangerous?"

"No, just demanding. I can handle bales of wool but not lambs."

"*Lambs?*"

"Two of them. They're always hungry and won't stay still. They wiggle like fish." He shuddered. "I nearly dropped one the other day."

His worry made her shake her head. The only better caregiver than him would be the lambs' own mothers. "Why do you have them?"

"My brothers brought them home with the wool from

the Merino farm. They were told it's early for lambs to be born, and these were..." His gaze dropped to his boots and stayed there.

"They were what?"

He ran his hand over the back of his neck, appearing reluctant to say more. "Orphans," he finally replied.

Like her and Wren, but maybe no longer Oriole. That's why he'd hesitated to say the word. He had another reason, though. He and his siblings were also orphans.

She scrambled for something to distract them both. "I assume the wool's for Robyn's husband. Does he know what you're bringing him?"

The mischief in his boyish grin made even the sun shine brighter. "It's a surprise."

The Llewellyn brothers loved to tease their brother-in-law and his family—especially Max's grandpa, Gus.

"It's our belated wedding present," Brynmor added. "We want Max to have the best wool so he can continue knitting gifts for our sister."

"And for you as well."

He shrugged. "If he wants, but what he really should do is sell his creations in Noelle and everywhere."

Max Peregrine was as stubborn as he was unusual, in the best ways. He'd welcomed her into his home even when his wife Robyn, at least at first, had not.

"I like the caps he knitted for you and your family." She especially liked that his cap couldn't contain his always neatly-trimmed auburn hair and how the dove-gray wool highlighted every shade of red and brown.

Instead of touching the hat on his head, his hand went to his pocket—and the older hat hidden there. He wouldn't give up the cap his father had given him, no matter how unraveled. "Max is as generous as he is busy. He and Robyn would gladly employ you again in the Noelle office. The letter you left with Mrs. Fitzpatrick, did it advise your sisters to go there if they needed help?"

"Of course." She may have mixed feelings about Mrs. Fitzpatrick, but she'd learned to trust the Peregrine family.

Plus their office and homes were conveniently situated across from the Noelle train depot. Her sisters wouldn't have to wander around Noelle looking for help. Or for her if she went back there.

"If we hurry, we might catch today's train to Noelle." Brynmor's stillness warred with his words. He appeared content to stay where he was.

But if they didn't make a move, she'd have to find a place to stay in Denver tonight. Whereas in Noelle, there was a room waiting for her and a paying job as well.

"Where are your lambs?" she asked.

"At my office."

"Since I've never been there, you'll have to lead the way."

He led only for the first few strides, then he matched her pace. He also maneuvered so his injured eye remained on his side farthest from her.

She'd missed seeing him. From every angle. Tomorrow, she'd be missing him again when she stayed in Noelle and he returned to Denver. She couldn't dwell on any of that. She needed to focus on her sisters.

"Before we leave, I'm giving your brothers money. Then if Oriole and Wren arrive, they'll have train fare to reach me." She didn't bother to correct her *if* to a *when*. No more wasting her time on that. She'd use Noelle as her base to hunt for her sisters in every nook and cranny of Denver. And its surrounding towns as well. She'd be purchasing a lot of train tickets. And, like Ulysses, she'd also promise to reward anyone who'd send her a telegram if they saw her sisters.

"My brothers won't take your money. Neither will I. We should've committed to helping you sooner, but..." Brynmor's unsaid words hung in the air between them.

But she hadn't let him.

And the moment it once again became too dangerous for him to be near her, she must change all of the plans she was making—and make sure Brynmor never saw her again.

CHAPTER 2

*B*alancing a fidgety lamb in one arm, Brynmor opened the railcar's door. Before he could take the other lamb from Lark, so she could more easily climb inside, she was aboard. As nimble as their foundlings' wild cousins who ruled Colorado's mountains.

She'd moved as fast as his sister. But Robyn had never, until recently, chosen to wear a dress. Lark must have lifted the hem of her striped skirt to aid her ascent. He hadn't noticed. He'd been looking elsewhere.

The ebony waterfall cascading down the back of her red jacket mesmerized him. He also hadn't noticed until he met Lark that most women tied up their hair. Lark was completely different from anyone he'd ever met. She didn't even braid her hair.

When she glanced over her shoulder, her dark eyes held a fathomless allure that rendered him speechless. "Have you changed your mind about traveling with me to Noelle?"

"No. Of course not." Why would she think that? *Because you're staring at her like a besotted fool rather than getting on the train with her.*

He tightened his grip on his cargo and followed her. A lot less gracefully. The lamb squirmed at the worst moment. Rather than let the rascal hit the wall, he let his shoulder take the brunt. "Ouch. You little b—" He gritted his teeth and patted the little bounder's head, trying to calm him.

"Are you all right?" Lark's silky voice soothed his agitation.

He lifted the lamb higher. It nestled its head under his chin and finally relaxed as well.

"Haven't felt this good in a long time." The truth in his words did not surprise him. He was with Lark. And he wasn't shirking his work, so he didn't have to feel guilty. At least not overly. He could've loaded the wool onto the train, put the lambs in Lark's excellent care, and trusted her and the conductor to handle the transport from there.

As was their routine, Robyn and Max would be waiting to unload their freight at the other end. He wasn't needed for that. But he wanted to be there to help with that. He wanted to hug his sister and see Max's reaction when he received his gift.

He wanted to see Lark's as well. Every second she stayed with him was *his* gift.

She watched him closely. One of her perfectly shaped eyebrows arched like a raven's wing. Was she finally ready to take flight? Away from not only his erratic behavior but all of him? He hid his eye by turning to close the railcar door behind him.

He didn't want her to run from him again. From his raging desire to be near her. From the flaw in his vision and in his character. He hadn't been strong enough to protect her.

When she'd first seen his murky eye, she'd appeared

horrified, but she hadn't turned her back on him. Instead, she clung to the false belief that she was responsible.

Only two people were to blame. Ulysses for wielding his lash and himself for not anticipating the rogue's assault.

He followed her along the narrow aisle to a pair of empty seats at the other end of the car. She'd wisely chosen the spot farthest from the other passengers. Here the lambs would be less likely to disturb anyone.

Her inky hair cut a compelling arc before settling out of sight behind her as she turned and sat with her spine straight against the rear wall.

He took the seat facing her. Or rather, facing the lamb sprawled on her lap. Her slender but strong hands—honed by a lifetime of playing music—cradled the imp, holding him safe. The same way she'd held him in Cheyenne when they danced, and he'd wondered if she'd—

The rising buzz of whispers yanked his focus from her.

When he glared over his shoulder, his gaze clashed with their fellow passengers' disapproving stares. Not for long. They ducked their heads and looked everywhere but at him. All too soon, they started sneaking glances at Lark and not the lamb in her arms.

Only the children watched the lambs, openly and with silent delight. He couldn't hear exactly what their elders continued whispering, but he'd heard enough from others to guess.

Brute-sized man with ugly white eye.

Beautiful woman with unfortunate heritage.

He'd given the last person who'd labeled her thus—along with other derogatory descriptions about *her kind*—the end of his fist. He'd finally earned the title of brute.

"They do not deserve to see you." Lark's voice was quiet but firm. "Give them your back."

When he did as she said, he found her staring out the window and not at their tormentors. Their scorn had most likely risen the instant he and Lark had entered the railcar. He'd been slow to notice, but she hadn't. She'd chosen the farthest seat for their lambs *and* him.

"I don't see Ulysses outside."

Her comment made him scan the platform in pursuit of her flamboyantly dressed troupe manager. On his second sweep of the lengthy walkway, he searched for anyone, in any outfit, who might be trying to conceal their identity.

The whistle blew, and the train chugged forward, leaving Denver and its worries behind.

Or not.

He held out his lamb for Lark to take. "Can you hold him as well? Just for a moment. I want to have a look at the second passenger car." He gestured behind him.

When she glanced in the direction he'd indicated, her frown became more worried than miffed. She'd picked their seats to keep them as far away from those they both could and couldn't see.

"Don't worry. If he got on without us noticing, he'll get more than he bargained for when he gets off in Noelle."

"You have faith in their sheriff?"

"Him and others. Many in Noelle judge people by their actions and not their appearance."

When her eyes narrowed on their fellow passengers, he regretted his words. He didn't care if they feared his size or were disturbed by his eye, but he cared how they made Lark feel.

She shrugged, collected his lamb, and leaned her head against the wall behind her. And began whispering, or rather humming, to their foundlings. Her voice rocked him like a lullaby.

He climbed slowly to his feet, finding it extremely difficult to walk away from her. He lifted the bag that held the bottled milk he'd brought for the lambs from his shoulder. Taking his time to prop it carefully in the corner of his seat made a good excuse to delay leaving her.

"I'll be fine on my own." She cocked her head as she gazed up at him. "With the train traveling this fast, I'm not going anywhere. And I've heard worse in my life."

He grunted, not liking her words, except for the part about not going anywhere. He strode toward the forward car. The sooner he completed his investigation, the sooner he could return to her.

When he did, he found her conversing in low tones with the industrious conductor who never stopped moving as he battled to keep the train on schedule...but who now occupied Brynmor's seat.

Caleb Court shot to his feet when he saw him approaching. "Brynmor. Mr. Llewellyn."

The formality doubled his tension. They'd been on a first-name basis for quite some time. Why was today different?

"I know I shouldn't be—" Caleb waved his hand as if at a loss for what he was doing. "I wanted to—" His face flushed a surprisingly bright shade of red. "I had to reassure Miss Lark that it was good to see her again. That she'll always be welcome on my train."

Jealousy crept up his spine. The boy was smitten.

But he was more than that. Brynmor sighed in acceptance. Caleb wasn't a boy. He was a young man, a hard worker, and a compassionate soul. Lark needed more people like Caleb near her.

"Thank you for your care." He held out his hand.

Caleb shook his hand without hesitation, but his youthfully lean body remained tense. "On behalf of the railroad, I must apologize for what's happened at the junction."

Brynmor groaned. An apology meant one thing. Their mutual concerns had come true. "It's not your fault. You warned us."

"What's happened?" Lark asked.

"The junction's attendant has gone missing," Caleb replied.

"Gone?" He'd thought the worst would be a longer than usual stretch of laziness. "For how long?"

"Long enough for the engineer and the boilerman to agree to shut down the water tower."

Brynmor fought the urge to pace the aisle like his brother would've done. Assuming Heddwyn's habits wouldn't help his situation or Lark's. Confusion and concern furrowed her brow.

He reclaimed his seat across from her so he could focus on his explanation. "Without someone tending the pump-house, the railroad's concerned about the tank and its pipes freezing."

"And you're worried because...?"

"Even though my family was informed of the station attendant's shortcomings—"

"I had to tell you," Caleb interrupted. "You needed to know the truth."

"And we thank you for your honesty." Brynmor shrugged. "The junction's location was too ideal not to take a chance on it. We hired the attendant to do the side job of setting up a hub for our freight. But without a functioning water tower, the train won't have a reason to stop. It'll take on water for its engine elsewhere."

Lark's gaze went from him to Caleb. "How long can you stop there today?"

"A few minutes. But if Mr. Llewellyn needs more time, I could—"

Brynmor raised his hand to halt where the conversation was heading. "I'm not getting off." *I'm not leaving Lark.* "I'll deal with the situation on my return trip."

Lark stared out the window at the world whipping by in a snowbound blur. "Do you think he departed of his own free will?"

She was asking if the man had been taken, probably worrying about her sisters suffering a similar fate. Was that how they'd become separated? She hadn't said, and he wasn't going to ask because no matter what had happened, Lark would be blaming herself for not keeping her family together. Better to focus on what lay ahead.

He tried to imagine who'd want the attendant enough to abduct him. Unfortunately, all he could envision was the man wandering into the woods and being unable to find his way back. Yesterday's snowfall would've erased his tracks.

He muttered a curse under his breath.

"Only Mr. Llewellyn can tell." Caleb's posture turned as rigid as when he'd risen to defend his reason for sitting with Lark.

He didn't like where the conversation was going again, but Lark's questioning gaze forced him to address it. "I know what's his and what's ours. When I handed over our stock, I assessed his living quarters and advised him how best to transform the space into an office. If his personal belongings are still at the junction, then he didn't plan his departure."

He'd wandered off or been taken. A search party would have to be organized.

"So there's really no choice," Lark said. "You must leave the train and check."

"And," Caleb added, "if Mr. Llewellyn decides he must

stay at the junction, I'll make sure, as always, that his cargo gets to Noelle without any hassles."

Apparently, the search party would be just him. "*Mr. Court*," he growled, "why don't you also take my seat again while I'm gone?" That suddenly all too real possibility spiked his jealousy but eased his worry. At least Lark wouldn't be alone for the remainder of her journey to Noelle.

Caleb nodded. "We have a plan. I'll notify the engineer and be back before the train stops." He left before Brynmor could argue or agree.

"Maybe," Lark said in a hopeful voice, "the attendant will have returned by the time we arrive."

"All of our lives, including his, would be easier if that happened." Job opportunities like this were rare and could set up a man for life. The secluded location was a minor hardship that wouldn't last long. A few months. Maybe a year. His frustration turned on himself.

Don't be so judgmental. You've never lived alone. He'd always had his brothers and sister with him. Until Robyn falling in love and getting married had broken up their quartet. He may have agreed to Robyn staying in Noelle with Max, but he'd never stop wishing his sister lived closer to him.

"Life," Lark said with a sigh, "would be much easier if there were more people like Mr. Court."

The fact that she hadn't used the conductor's first name eased his agitation. She'd never once called him Mr. Llewellyn. That was what she called his brothers on the few occasions she'd spoken to them in Cheyenne—in a tone as reserved as theirs when they'd spoken to Lark and her sisters.

His entire family's standoffishness had been peculiar. Luckily, in Noelle, they'd all mellowed.

"I hoped I wasn't wrong in taking a chance on him," Lark murmured as she petted the lambs nestled against her.

Lucky little bounders. He cleared his throat grudgingly. The rascals deserved all of her affection after being orphaned. "A chance on him? Or them? You mean the lambs?"

"You're a terrible teaser." Her smile made his heart race and his clothes feel too tight.

He crossed his arms and tried to sit still. "Am I?"

"I'm not the only one who's mentioned the Llewellyn brothers' humor."

But you're the one whose opinion suddenly means the most. "If we're not discussing the lambs, then who are we talking about?"

"The conductor."

"And what *chance* did you take on him?" He didn't like how that sounded.

Her back stiffened in response to his gruff tone. "I asked him to watch for my sisters."

"Oh."

"*Oh* what?" she snapped.

He shrugged. "I should've asked him to help you. You can trust him."

The tension drained from her body as she leaned back against her seat. "If that's the case, then why were you scowling at him like a bear?"

He scrubbed his hand over his face, wanting to erase that moment and the jealousy that kept rising with each mention of the young man. When he glimpsed the shadow of a smile on her lips, he dropped his hand so he could inspect her more closely. "Are you sure you aren't the terrible teaser?"

She raised her eyebrows as if his question were outlandish. Her tactic failed because it only drew his attention to her eyes, which shone with— He inhaled sharply. Her dark eyes danced with happiness, unfettered by any torment, including rage and remorse. A rare sight he'd glimpsed precious few times.

"I'm speaking the truth." The huskiness in her voice made his blood pound in his veins.

"Uh-huh." He cleared his throat and strove to speak coherently. "And when did you last see a bear? Let alone a scowling bear?"

"The answer to both of your questions is..." She shrugged. "It's been a while. Which makes my description even more fitting because I almost never see you scowl either."

Was she deliberately teasing him to distract him from his worries? What about hers? They may have retreated, but they weren't gone.

"I'm sorry."

Her lips parted with surprise. "For what?"

"Like I said. I should've enlisted Court's help sooner."

"Thank you."

"For what?" He grimaced. Echoing her words made him sound little better than a parrot. His ability to banter had flown to the far heavens.

"For always wanting to help me. Even after I snap at you for doing so. Even when you have your own challenges clamoring for your attention. Like this..." She stared out the window as if seeking the right words as well. "What is it called? Junction Town?"

"It's too small to be a town and too new to have a name.

For now, it's simply *the junction*." He reached for his lamb, ready to do his part again.

She shook her head. "I'll hold them so you'll have both hands free to jump off at the junction. And back on, too. Don't go bashing into any more walls."

He snorted a laugh. "I'll try."

"You'd better do more than that. I don't want you getting hurt again." She reached out to touch his shoulder, the one he'd bumped against the train while getting on. "I want—" Her hand and her gaze plummeted to the lambs.

He leaned toward her but stopped short of touching her as well. He set his elbows on his knees and let his hands hang in the space separating them. "What do you want?"

She exhaled a long breath full of melancholy but also mischief. "To hear what you'll say when you give Barnum and Bailey to your brother-in-law and sister."

"Who are Barnum and Bailey?"

"They're famous circus showmen that I read about. And, since trying to hold on to two lively lambs probably feels like containing a circus sometimes, I figured they were excellent names for these little ones." When she scratched both Barnum and Bailey behind their ears, they wriggled in bliss, and he couldn't help but laugh.

His worries over his words, what to say and not say, vanished. Lark had never judged him, and speaking about everything and nothing with her was a routine he was eager to resume. Their time in Cheyenne suddenly seemed like yesterday, not hundreds of days ago. All too soon, the train began to slow.

No. He'd imagined it. They weren't nearing his stop. He still had time to—

At the other end of their railcar, Caleb's arrival announced his departure. "We're making a short stop to let one man off. There's nothing outside worth seeing, so stay inside. If you disembark, you'll be left behind. You'll freeze your toes off waiting for the next train. And it won't be here until tomorrow, going in the opposite direction, heading back to Denver."

Despite the dire warning, Lark smiled. "When there's work to be done, I can't imagine you standing still long enough to suffer even a nip of frostbite."

"If I stayed at the junction till the next train arrived, I wouldn't stop until I had the office set up and enough wood chopped to warm myself for a fortnight." He shook his head. "Not me. The attendant. The one I should've picked rather than trusting the railroad." A rush of certainty made him sit up straight. "That's the answer."

"What is?"

"Get the junction ready, then choose the next man myself."

"After you find out what happened to the first one."

He slumped back in his seat. "Yes, after I do that. And everything else."

"You'll succeed. Of that I've no doubt. Your junction will become a thriving part of the business you've worked so hard to build. It's only unfortunate you must tackle today's endeavor alone."

But he wouldn't be alone for long. He had family at both ends of the line. While she had no idea where her sisters were or if she'd ever see them again. "After I search the junction, we can—" The chances of them being a *we* were diminishing. He didn't want to set one foot off this train.

"Better hurry." Her voice turned husky as she said in a rush, "Or you won't make it back to tell me what your investigation reveals." She faced the window, and her lips formed a thin line.

He knew that look. She was determined not to say another word.

He covered the distance to the rear door in two strides. Outside, he braced himself on the step. The frosty wind whipped his face, but not his scalp or his ears—thanks to a fine sheep and an even finer brother-in-law who'd transformed a ball of yarn into a much-needed cap. Max and Robyn would take good care of Lark, but he wanted to be the one to do the caring. He shook his head at his selfish thoughts.

You haven't the luxury to do everything you want.

When the train slowed just enough, he leapt off. He hit the bank running, straight for the junction's single lodging, an abandoned cabin only discovered by chance when the track was laid nearby.

If the junction survived, a new building would be needed, closer to the tracks and double, or even triple, in size. The snow lay heaped against the cabin's sturdy but rustic log walls, climbing higher with each gust of wind.

A flurry came inside with him. He slammed the door shut to clear his sightline.

Not that he needed to see very far. The room was small and square, and empty of human life. It was, however, still full of the crates and sacks he'd left with the attendant.

He threaded his way through the freight. Easily. Nothing had been unpacked or even opened. No personal items lay scattered about either.

He pressed his palm to the potbelly stove. Stone cold.

Inspired by Lark's letter leaving at the music shop, he searched for a note. Which turned out to be another waste of his time. People left letters when they cared. This man most certainly did not. His assumption made him sigh.

You know precious little about the man. So stop being judgmental.

He reviewed the room one last time and ended up facing the back door.

What if the attendant had hurt himself outside and hadn't been able to make it back inside?

He yanked open the door and stepped into pristine snow disturbed only by his footprints and the tip of a wooden handle. Hellfire! The man had left an axe on the ground where someone might've stepped on it?

He grabbed the handle and whacked the blade into the nearest block of wood. The man wouldn't have had to go far to put it there. The meager hump of wood stacked against the back of the cabin spoke of more idleness. So did the cords hidden under the snow. He stubbed his toes on several as he made his way around the back of the cabin, examining the trees for a clue to where the attendant might have gone.

The steam whistle shattered the hushed stillness. His time was up.

He sprinted toward the train, gazing down its length in pursuit of the last railcar. The spot where he'd hop back on and see Lark again.

Behind the engine, the wood tender was stacked high with fuel. The link between it and the first passenger car was occupied as well. A man shrouded from shoulder to shin in a bulky coat drew back, disappearing into the shadow of the wood car. The swiftness of his departure made the white in his dark hair flash. The coloring marked him as Ulysses T. Stone.

"Son of a trickster," Brynmor growled. "That's where you've been hiding?"

The train chugged forward. He raced for Lark's railcar and leapt onto the platform behind it. Holding tight to the railing, he leaned out as far as he could and locked his gaze on the forward cars. He forced himself not to blink. He waited to see if Ulysses would show himself again.

No one of any description appeared. They were all headed to Noelle. And after they got there? Perhaps Lark shouldn't stay in Noelle. Not with Ulysses there and him having to return to Denver. After they delivered Barnum and Bailey, she should come home with him.

The railcar door burst open. With a lamb clutched in each arm, Lark ran straight for him. Her eyes wide. Her face ghostly pale.

Dread iced his veins. "What's wrong?"

"Come with me." She thrust Barnum into his arms and jumped off the train.

He tightened his grasp on the lamb and leapt after her. He hadn't a hope of catching her and halting her fall. Heck, he'd be lucky if he didn't land flat on his face.

Lark's feet hit the ground without a mishap. She didn't even stumble. Astoundingly, neither did he.

But why had she jumped? Who was chasing her? Where was Caleb? When he glanced back at the train, he found the conductor standing in the doorway that Lark had practically flown through.

"Don't blame him." Lark words hit him with the wind. "I ordered him to open the door for me."

With the train now picking up speed as it continued down the track away from them, it was hard to see, but Caleb's expression appeared as confused as Brynmor felt. The young man raised his hand and gave him a brisk salute.

The jaunty farewell did nothing to slow the thundering beat of his heart.

The train rounded the bend and was gone.

When he turned in search of Lark, she was gone as well. But the door to the cabin stood wide open.

CHAPTER 3

*B*rynmor hovered in the cabin doorway, gaping at her as if she'd gone mad.

She wanted him to think well of her, but not at the expense of his well-being. "Mr. Court told me he'd seen something odd. And I—" She struggled for the word to describe the oddness of what had happened to her. She hugged Bailey tighter. "I panicked."

Brynmor's eyebrows rose even higher. She had trouble comprehending it as well. The moment he'd left, a coldness had invaded her. But as she'd watched him return, her fear had chilled her to the bone.

That had to be insanity.

When she shivered, he closed the door, handed her Barnum, and went straight to the stove. "Until I get the fire going, hold them close. You'll conserve heat together."

She shifted her weight from one foot to the other, trying to warm up that way as well. Why was it so much colder here than in Denver? *It's just the elevation, silly. You're in the mountains. This is nothing new.*

But being alone in a tiny room with Brynmor was.

The stove's hinges squeaked, wood clunked against metal, and a match hissed. Against that industrious clatter, Brynmor's voice flowed like a calming brook as he asked, "What happened after Court shared his odd story?"

"I told him I had to get off the train, that I was afraid for my safety." She sucked in a breath and then blurted, "He'd seen Ulysses."

Brynmor nodded but didn't raise his gaze from the stove. "He must've seen him as he made his way forward to speak with the engineer about our stop."

"How did you know?" She pressed her cheeks against both lambs, taking comfort in their soft wool and warmth. "Did you see Ulysses as well?"

"Only from a distance. Did Court question him? What excuse did Ulysses make for not being in a passenger car?"

"He'd been sickened by the sight of something and needed fresh air." Those words usually meant he suffered from a severe case of yearning to trounce someone.

Brynmor huffed. "The air's not so fresh behind an engine's smokestack."

"That's what Mr. Court said. Then Ulysses presented his ticket with an aggressiveness that didn't suit anyone, ill or not. Luckily, their conversation ended there." Her stomach still rolled with fear for the young conductor who'd shown her kindness. Ulysses had bragged many times about throwing men who'd displeased him under moving trains.

"What happened next?"

"I didn't want to face his anger again, so I jumped." She pressed her lips tight, ending her story there. Let him think she had been most afraid for herself.

"Or..." Brynmor doffed his wool cap and raked his fingers through his hair. The soft glow from the growing fire turned the thick auburn waves even redder. "You didn't want me to face him again."

She'd accomplished that. Her stubbornly helpful Welsh giant was safe. And without her near him, Mr. Court hopefully was safe as well.

Her shivers lessened, and her bravado returned. She raised her chin. "Or I never liked watching from the wings. Now I can see what you discovered in this cabin."

"You'll see nothing." His long sigh left a ghostly trail in the air. "The attendant's belongings are gone. He didn't even stay long enough to make a dent in the food supplies we'd left him."

"Good news. He left with intent, and there's no need to search for him. You can stay here." *With me.*

He grabbed several blankets from a nearby stack and arranged them on the floor by the stove.

"What are you doing?"

"Making a nest for our lambs."

Our. Her heart thudded as she savored the silent echo in her soul. "How cozy," she murmured, trying not to appear undone by a single word. When she placed Barnum and Bailey on their bed, her arm brushed Brynmor's, and her body flushed with heat.

"Everything in here is snug," he muttered as he stepped back to give her room. Or at least tried.

She set the bag—that she'd slung over her shoulder before bolting from the train—on the floor, took out two bottles of milk, and handed one to Brynmor. They both knelt to feed the suddenly *very* wiggly lambs.

Barnum and Bailey's eagerness to guzzle every drop consumed her attention. They rocked forward and back, bouncing against the bottles as they enjoyed their feast. Their darling eyes widened, their impish tails wagged, and their spindly legs quivered. When they finished, they flopped down on their bed and curled up close to each other, becoming one enticingly fluffy ball of wool.

No matter how cute they were, she couldn't stare at them all night. She turned her gaze to the clutter in the cabin so she wouldn't be tempted to stare at Brynmor all night as well.

"If you see a feed sack," he said, "let me know. When Barnum and Bailey wake up, they might enjoy some ground corn."

The corner of a familiar shape caught her eye. She wound her way through the freight to get a better look. "Of all the things to have in an office, and one this size, why is a piano here?"

"Forgot about that." His gaze fell to his hands, twisting his cap like they needed to keep busy. He shoved the hat in his pocket and opened the nearest crate and began removing items. "Our hired man insisted on it."

"You bought a piano for him? Why?"

"Because he spoke about music the way you did." He shrugged. "Guess it wasn't as important as he said."

"What did he say?"

"That..." He kept working as he pondered the answer. *"Silence is deafening, and music speaks volumes."*

"All that effort to accommodate him, and he still abandoned his post?" She lifted the fallboard, pressed several keys, and grimaced. "Out of tune." She snuck a peek at him and longed to tease the frown from his brow. "Maybe that's why your man left."

When his shoulders hunched, she regretted her words. He looked like the unhappy bear she'd compared him to when he'd found her talking to the conductor. "If you knew, I have no doubt you'd have arranged its repair quickly."

"I would've brought Mrs. Fitzpatrick here." He heaved one of his all too familiar sighs as he studied the room. "If she were agreeable. This isn't going to be a comfortable place for you to stay."

"Are you the same man who said he could set up this office in a—?"

"I'm too distracted." He stopped unloading the crate. The contents had gone from neatly stacked inside to a jumble on the floor.

"By thoughts of Ulysses? We're free of him until the train returns tomorrow. He's headed to Noelle without us."

"How do you know he's not jumping off somewhere along the line?"

"He won't. Not at full steam or even as a train is picking up speed. Nearly broke his ankle doing that. Even Ulysses has his weaknesses."

"Good to know." His voice rumbled with relief, but not for long. "And when he doesn't see us get off in Noelle?"

"He'll assume we're hiding and scour the train and then the town. We should warn your sister. We'll telegraph Noelle."

"That's not possible."

"Why? Outside there's a pole with wires and inside—" She reviewed the room until understanding made her halt. "Is the telegraph machine in one of these crates?" she asked hopefully.

He did a quick search. "In here." He tapped the top of one. "But finding it doesn't help much because I haven't a clue how to use it."

"Our missing man had those skills?"

He shrugged. "So he said."

"Well, Mr. Court will tell Robyn and the Peregrines

where we are. A real conversation is as good as any highfa-lutin' wires."

"Highfalutin'?" His scowl vanished. The strength of his grin made her heart skip a beat. "You sound like Grandpa Gus."

"Why, thank you," she said primly, trying to conceal how much she enjoyed making him smile. "Gus is an open-minded man, a compassionate soul, and a patient teacher." There'd been a dearth of all three at the orphanage. She pried her thoughts away from her sour past and fixed them on the sassy sweetness in one man. "Gus is...the grandfather I always dreamed of having."

"Me too."

Brynmor had been only a boy when life had made him the eldest in his family. As far as she could see, he'd been an exceptionally fine father figure for his siblings, but it couldn't have been easy.

She had to clear the tightness from her throat before she could speak. "I enjoyed working with Gus in Noelle."

"And Robyn and Max enjoyed knowing you were keeping Gus occupied." Brynmor studied the room as if it confused him as much as it might have muddled their elderly friend. "Setting up this office isn't going to be as easy as I said. Like Gus, my mind's gone wandering." He moved to peer out the window. He didn't have to go far. "It'll be dark soon. I'll have to go out and fix the woodpile."

If she were Oriole, she'd spend her time inside trying to fix the piano. After meeting Mrs. Fitzgerald, Oriole had become obsessed with repairing instruments. A hard trade to learn without an instructor.

Since leaving Ulysses, Lark had found quite a few people willing to teach her new things. What kind of teacher would Brynmor be? He'd been a fine student.

Showing him how to dance had been remarkably easy and thoroughly enjoyable.

"In Noelle, Grandpa Gus taught me how to run his post office. He said his grandsons had organized everything to work the most efficiently. Before you go, will you share your plans for your new office with me?"

He did and ended with, "It's as much a general store as a freight office. Everything we need to stay for a night, or even a month, is in this room."

A month with him? In this snug space? The idea made her mind race with possibilities.

"We even have a piano." She made a show of gesturing to it, hoping the sweep of her arm would conceal the truth. She'd lost her once ironclad self-control. She couldn't stop craving more time with him while worrying what would happen if they stayed together too long. Or parted ways too quickly, and she couldn't stop Ulysses from hurting him again.

"I'd rather have a hurdy-gurdy." His gaze pinned her, feeding her hopes that he was talking about more than the instrument.

"You like the gurdy that much?"

"Only when you're playing it." He strode for the back door but paused with his hand on the latch. "I'm sorry I haven't provided more. That..." He heaved a sigh. "That this room isn't larger."

"It's bigger than most places I've lived, and I've always thought cozy homes were the best. They keep people together."

Had he thought about that? Them having to sleep here *alone together*? Just the two of them. Without any walls between them.

CHAPTER 4

*S*tanding in the dark room, outside the circle of firelight, Brynmor's heart pounded, chaotic as a hundred drums, as he watched Lark doing what he hadn't been able to stop thinking about. Not once since he'd stood in the cabin doorway and seen her in this tiny room.

She was defining where they would sleep.

She nudged her bedroll, her share of the pile of wool blankets they'd found in the freight, closer to the stove. He clutched his blanket tighter to his chest, then shifted the material lower for better coverage. Not even half an hour of vigorous wood chopping had softened his ardor.

Finally, she stopped fidgeting with the placement of her bed. She took a seat on it and patted the space beside her. "Is this enough room for you?"

"Yes." His reply came out rough, from a mouth as dry as the dust they'd swept from the room. He was lucky he'd uttered even one word.

"Are you sure?" She surveyed the cabin. "I could try to make more room if you need it."

He said nothing and stayed still, waiting for her to decide what she needed.

"I think this is the best layout." She picked up the brush they'd also found in the freight.

He'd insisted she keep it for herself. When she'd resisted, he'd told her to consider it part of the compensation she'd receive for setting up the office. A task they'd completed, but only after working late into the night.

"You've made everything look..." The stroke of the brush over her glossy hair made him forget what he'd been saying. There was only her. And she looked— "Perfect."

She shrugged one shoulder, elegantly and very enticingly. "I did what you suggested. And worked for less than an hour on my own before you returned and helped me finish."

It'd been a struggle to stay away even that long. He preferred working beside her. He'd have to sort out the woodpile in the morning.

She set her brush carefully beside her blankets, as if it were her most cherished possession—until she fixed her attention on her watch and studied it closely. "Aren't you tired? It's past midnight."

He'd never get tired of gazing upon her. But it appeared he'd have to start acting tired if he wanted her to get any sleep.

He placed his bed beside hers as carefully as she'd set down her brush, making sure he stayed squarely on his side of their sleeping space. From the corner of his good eye, he watched her stretch out on her side, her elbow propped on her blankets, her palm cradling her head.

He sat facing the stove and fiddled with the kindling, trying to keep his own hands occupied.

"Are you cold?" she asked.

He shook his head. "Are you? I can get more wood."

"We have more than enough right here."

He felt the same way, but he wanted her to have more than a bedroll, a brush, and a watch. "You haven't had many luxuries in your life."

"Oh, but I have." She stared at Barnum and Bailey sleeping nearby, nestled together on their shared blankets.

Lucky little bounders.

"I had my sisters with me for fourteen years. And we had our music, both shared and separate."

"When is music separate?"

"We've always performed as a trio. By choice and not because Ulysses insisted. But we've often chosen to practice on our own." She smiled as she studied the room again. "Even in spaces smaller than this. Each of us has always had a private affair with a special instrument."

"I never saw you play one more than another. Except for your hurdy-gurdy." And then one day she didn't have it anymore. When he'd asked why, she'd said she'd sold it to a man who'd liked the sound of it. "I never understood how you could let it go."

"Because the man wanted the gurdy and when I refused, Ulysses said he'd sell everything I had if the price was right. When the deal was done, the man came to me and offered to return the gurdy if I spent the night with him."

His heart seized with rage. At the man and Ulysses and himself. He'd been in Cheyenne when this happened. What else had she hidden from him back then? "Why didn't you tell me?"

"I couldn't. It was a test. Ulysses was always seeking something that might break the vow I'd made."

"What vow?"

"After our first week with Ulysses, I swore if he ever forced me or my sisters to sleep with men for his profit, I'd strangle him with a string from Oriole's violin. They were actually Wren's words. But she only whispered them to me and Oriole, and now that I think on it, I believe she used *garrote* not *strangle*."

"Holy Moses." He couldn't imagine Lark's timid and tiny sister doing that, let alone saying she would. Wren hadn't said a word to him.

"Growing up in a French mission surrounded by an endless river of transient fur traders changes one's vocabulary. And perceptions. If I'd accepted the man's offer, it would've been a choice. I would not have been forced."

"You were coerced," he growled. "And bullied and—"

She held up her hand. "Letting go of my gurdy was the only way to show I remained fully committed to my sisters."

"But you still could've told me. I would've helped you keep your vow *and* your gurdy too."

"And been thrown in jail for your troubles. Cheyenne was Ulysses' Utopia. He always found ways to make their lawmen do what he wanted."

Her continued excuses for not sharing her life with him fueled his frustration. "What about Oriole's violin?" he demanded. "It's important to her, and she still has it."

A frown pinched her brow. "Her violin is...unique. It's important to all of us. Even Ulysses. We've always treated it differently, and I—" She exhaled wearily. "I stopped asking why."

"Maybe the *difference* was Oriole decided she'd fight for everything she loved."

When Lark flinched, he did as well. Self-reproach

stabbed him. He'd been gallingly judgmental today. First the station attendant, and now her.

He met her gaze squarely. "I shouldn't have said that. I'm sorry."

"I'm sorry as well." Her voice was hushed, but not hesitant. "For many things I've said."

But she'd only said them because she'd faced more challenges than he could ever imagine. She'd been fighting for herself and her sisters long before they met Ulysses. The only pleasant thing she'd ever mentioned about the orphanage was being allowed to sing and play music, mostly at services in church. The mission had been heavy-handed in its quest to assimilate children with native blood.

And him? Was he trying to change her to suit him as well?

When he'd first seen her gently chiding Wren, he'd been intrigued. When she'd spun to face him, he'd been spellbound. Her unbound hair had whipped around her with the force of her turn. Every muscle in her slender body had straightened, making her appear taller. And her eyes had flashed like obsidian daggers.

She'd been the bear she'd teased him about being. Fierce, protective, untamed. If she hadn't told him to never come near her again, he would've been content to catch a glimpse of her occasionally in Cheyenne. He wouldn't have asked for more.

Liar. You craved so much more. You still do.

Her head tilted at an inquisitive angle as she watched him. Was she questioning his stillness? Had she sensed his thoughts?

Silence wasn't his friend. He cleared his throat. "We all fight in our own way." His words came easily, with conviction. "Even Wren."

"I'll do whatever it takes to guard her and Oriole. And you too." She folded her arms. "The gurdy had to go. As did you."

"Me? You told me to leave in order to protect your sisters *and me?*" He shook his head vigorously, then lowered his chin belligerently. "*Telling* me to leave won't work again."

"I didn't think it would. That's why I'm trying to tell you something different. *The truth.*" Her brows arched, challenging him to disagree. "It all comes down to one thing. My life isn't mine to live freely. And neither is yours. Your first priority must be staying safe so you can help your family."

Her words made him shake his head again. "This isn't like it was in Cheyenne or all the places I lived before that. I've had the time and good fortune to settle my family into a prosperous life and then accept that I must let them go. Wherever they decide is best. I'm no longer a brother trying to be a parent. And Rob, Hedd, and Griff are all the stronger because I've changed and so have they."

Speaking of his family made him remember something. He pulled the letter from his pocket and held it out to her.

When her eyes widened much too hopefully, he rushed to explain. "It's not from your sisters. My brother wrote it. Said I was supposed to give it to you as soon as we had a quiet moment to think." Then he'd been distracted by Ulysses, the train passengers, Caleb, the missing station attendant, and, of course, her. Always her.

She took the letter but didn't open it. She stared at it like it might swallow her whole. "That sounds like something Griffin would say. He's always mulling over things, but why would he write to me?"

Mulling, or brooding as Robyn called it, was one of the few ways Griffin had found to stifle his temper. But he wasn't the brother in question. "The letter's from Heddwyn."

Her jaw dropped in surprise. He shared her amazement. His middle brother couldn't stand still. Heddwyn had never let a quiet moment remain quiet.

When she finally opened the letter, he lay down on his bedroll and stared at the ceiling. She deserved more privacy, but his legs refused to put any distance between them again.

After a long moment, she said, "You didn't read it."

The certainty in her voice drew his gaze to her. She pulled her notebook from her pocket, tucked Heddwyn's letter inside, and set it beside her brush and watch.

"He said you'd share it with me when you were ready."

"Are you sure he said *when* and not *if*?" Before he could answer, she said, "If I don't get a chance to see him again in Denver, please tell him I appreciate the time he took to write to me."

He grunted. He'd forgotten about having to return to that city in the morning.

"You're scowling again. Over a letter as kind as it was thoughtful." Lark lay down on her bedroll and stared at the ceiling, mirroring his pose. Except only a fading frown—or a suppressed one—disturbed her brow.

Heddwyn was capable of great kindness, but he hadn't shown it in Cheyenne.

He tried to sound unconcerned as he said, "I was thinking about tomorrow."

She nodded slowly. "We...can't stay here." A hard edge replaced the waver in her voice. "There's no place to hide or run to if things get bad. When the train arrives, we should assume Ulysses will be on it. We board before he can get off. We avoid a confrontation."

"Agreed." Then, as soon as the train left the junction, he'd do his own confronting. But not in Denver or Noelle, where his family might be pulled into the strife. He'd delayed his fight with Ulysses too long.

This time he'd ask Caleb to take his seat with Lark before he—

He fought the tightness in his throat and forced himself to accept what he must do. He must walk away from Lark and search every part of the train, inside and out, and battle her troupe manager alone.

CHAPTER 5

Under a cloudless blue sky that reminded her of Brynmor's uninjured eye, Lark leaned against the front of the cabin and studied the infamous water tower that had led her Welshman to depart the train. Behind the cabin, the repetitive thump of Brynmor's axe sang to her, telling her where he was and how hard he worked. A softer chorus of thunks marked his breaks to stack the split wood, building the pile high enough to reach the roof—as he'd informed her was his goal.

In Cheyenne, he'd told her he'd never lived in the wilderness, but he'd spent most of his time outdoors. His days had been filled with driving wagons and caring for the horses or mules that pulled them. That activity plus loading and unloading the freight had turned him into a mountain of muscle with a humble core.

The down-to-earth tones of his current labor soothed her. The crisp, clean winter air allowed her to breathe deeply. A pleasant change from the many strident saloons and moldy boardinghouses that had structured her song-bird life.

Despite having little sleep, everything at the junction invigorated her. She couldn't stop hoping Brynmor felt the same. His tossing and turning—after their conversation ended last night—didn't, however, bode well for their feelings being in tune.

She scanned the trees set back from the track to create an open but still sheltered spot. The plump spruce and barren aspens, which would be adorned with golden leaves in the fall, held hidden potential. In those woods and beyond lived many loggers, ranchers, and even a few trappers who could benefit from their goods being transported in and out by train. If the station attendant had the energy, the service could even be extended by packhorse or by wagon as roads were established.

This junction had a future.

It'd be a fine place to put down roots, to make a forever home. But Brynmor's office and his brothers were in Denver, a booming city with an even bigger abundance of work. Any savvy business owner—not to mention dedicated family man—would focus on that and hire someone else to stay here.

As Brynmor had done. Or tried to do.

A whistle echoed faintly in the distance. The chopping on the other side of the cabin halted abruptly.

Her hands shook as she checked her watch. The train was ahead of its scheduled time. Either that, or it was right on time, and Mr. Court was giving them plenty of warning. Had the conductor once again seen Ulysses onboard?

Her imperfect past barreled toward her, threatening to ruin her perfect reprieve with the man she loved.

She rushed back inside the cabin. On the other side of the room, Brynmor came in through the rear door with equal speed.

"Are our lambs ready to go?"

His continued use of the word *our* filled her with joy. So did the sight of their foundlings bolting toward him. The little darlings bounded around him, then butted his shins with their tiny heads. He scooped them up, one in each arm.

When they wriggled rather than relaxing in his hold, he grimaced and hurried across the room toward her. "Why do they still dislike me?"

"Are you joking? They adore you." She felt the same way.

He halted beside her. His scowl eased to a dubious frown as his gaze went from his cargo to her. "Then why are they squirming to get away?"

"They're not. They're trying to get closer." When she touched his arms, he tensed as usual. This time she didn't pull back. "If they wiggle, try holding them closer. Or actually higher." She nudged his arms upward.

As soon as Barnum and Bailey's heads touched the bottom of Brynmor's chin, they nuzzled him and finally relaxed.

So did he. He sighed deeply as he whispered, "It's a miracle."

"Enjoy it while it lasts. This is the first time they've held still all morning."

"They're making up for barely moving a hoof all night. I'm glad you got settled and could sleep as well."

She may have lain still, but she hadn't slept after their conversation ended. With Brynmor beside her, she hadn't been tired. Her soul sang whenever he was near.

They stood very close now. Her gaze dropped to her hands, still touching his arms. She had to let go. This interlude had to end. They couldn't stay here. But these last hours would remain forever in her heart. She'd spent more time alone with him than she had ever dared hope for.

And she had Heddwyn's letter that might lead to more. Her mind kept humming Brynmor's hyperactive brother's words like a new song that was fast becoming her favorite.

My brother needs you. Stay with him.

Stay with all of us. All of the Llewellyns and the Peregrines too.

I want to protect you and your sisters. I vow that I will. But I can do nothing from a distance. And hardly anything on my own.

Stand still with me.

Could it be done? Could she accept Heddwyn's request? Would their combined families prosper if she stood still and stayed with Brynmor?

The train whistle came again. A long, clear blast. Brynmor went out the front door. After one final glance at the cabin, which felt more like a home than an office, she followed him and closed the door behind her.

"When the train arrives," Brynmor said as they walked toward the track, "we'll board as fast as we can."

Without breaking stride, she took Bailey from him. "Tell the engineer not to stop."

He nodded. "If they slow down just enough, we can jump on."

"And if Ulysses appears, we sidestep him and keep moving until we're in a passenger car again."

"I thought you said that safety in numbers was an illusion."

"I'm reconsidering. Perhaps it all depends on who's making up the numbers."

They halted together beside the track. The train rounded

the bend, slowing its approach. Mr. Court stood on the platform between the wood tender and the first passenger car, the same spot where he'd said he'd seen Ulysses yesterday. The conductor waved, then shouted something that was muffled by the churning wheels and pistons.

Brynmor's sigh rumbled with foreboding. "Looks like he can't wait to talk to us."

Mr. Court yelled again, and this time his words rose above the racket. "Sorry! I didn't see him until it was too late."

"Can't be helped," Brynmor yelled back. "We'll board at your position." He turned to the engineer who'd poked his head out of the cab's window. "No need to stop. Keep her slow, and we'll climb aboard."

When he stepped behind her, she swung to face him. "What are you doing?"

"Letting you jump on first."

"But—"

"You're better at this than me." He nudged her shoulder until she faced the train again. "Show me how, and I promise I'll be right behind you."

Mr. Court stepped back to clear a space for them. "After we left Noelle, I found—"

"Me." A thin but spry man with carrot-colored hair filled the space beside the conductor.

"Grandpa Gus," Lark gasped. "Why are you here?"

"I came to see what yer doing."

"Step back, Mr. Peregrine," the younger man ordered. "As soon as they board, we're leaving."

"Leavin'? But I just got here." Gus shook his head so briskly he sent his flat cap askew. "And who you callin' *mister*? I told you to call me Grandpa."

"And I've already told you why we can't stay here. Now step back."

Gus' jaw took a mulish tilt. "Never. I gotta see what's goin' on."

Their boarding spot, along with the bickering duo, edged past them.

Brynmor nudged her shoulder again. "Use the next platform."

As it arrived, she tightened her grip on Bailey, sucked in a breath, and leapt.

"Why ain't this train stoppin'?" Gus roared. "Do you expect me to jump off?"

Her feet hit the bottom step. She hastened up toward the others to give Brynmor room to follow her. When his weight jarred the iron behind her, her breath left her in a relieved whoosh.

They'd made it. They were safe, and the train was again picking up speed.

"*Grandpa Gus*," Mr. Court shouted as if horrified. "Don't you dare."

"I'm gettin' off *now!*" Gus' final word soared like a bird in flight.

Lark swung around. Gus shot from his perch like a cannonball and hit the earth like a rolling stone.

"Stop the train!" she yelled in unison with Brynmor and Mr. Court.

Brynmor jumped down. She did as well. They both raced to Gus' side.

"Grandpa?" Brynmor's whisper mirrored the dread in her heart. "How badly are you hurt?"

The old-timer scrambled nimbly to his feet. "Why would I be hurt? The last time I got off a train, I landed the same way 'n I was just fine." He cocked his head as he studied the train that was grinding to a stop. "But that day the train was kind enough to have halted first."

"We need to hurry and get back on." Brynmor gestured for Gus to follow them.

Gus did everything but that. He straightened his flat cap, smoothed his beard, then swept the snow from his clothing. "Why is everyone in such an all-fired hurry today? Yesterday, Caleb was in absolutely no rush when he informed us that you two had stayed here. A lot of words were said." He shrugged. "Most of them I can't remember, so I had to see fer myself."

A disquieting thought rose in Lark's mind. "Does anyone know you left Noelle?"

"I'll tell 'em when I get back. Is that the new freight office?" Gus headed toward the cabin. "Its logs look older than me."

Lark snared his sleeve. "Grandpa, we can't stay."

Gus' gaze went from her fingers gripping his coat to her arm cradling her lamb. "Are you starting a sheep farm?"

Behind Lark, the end of the now-reversing train gently chugged to a stop, completely at odds with the discord marking the train's first appearance—until a booming voice demanded, "This is the place you said would interest me?"

A stern-faced man sporting a tailored frock coat and overgrown mutton-chop sideburns stood on the rear step of the last railcar. The red caboose hadn't been part of the train when it departed Denver.

"*This,*" the gentleman repeated with even more disdain, "rustic shambles is what I moved my impeccable private car for?"

Lark bristled in defense of her junction. She shook her head. *The* junction. It wasn't hers. She may feel a kinship to this place, but she had no ownership over anything. That didn't matter. The junction may be rustic, but it wasn't in a shambles.

And who was this blowhard to cast judgment, anyway? She'd heard of railroad investors converting cabooses to living quarters in order to travel in style, but while this man's car may be *private*, it most certainly was not *impeccable*. The hasty paint job couldn't conceal the weathered wood.

She stiffened even more when a second windbag joined the first and launched into a familiar showman's speech. "'Tis not the place but the performer." Ulysses gestured to her. "And there she is. My lead songbird. Ready to entertain you and your associates."

"She," Brynmor shot back, "doesn't have to sing for you or anyone."

"But she will." Ulysses opened his enormous, and most likely illegally gained, fur coat to reveal his usual dandified clothing and planted his palms on his hips.

His purposefully distracting posturing filled her with unease. What hidden card was he waiting to play?

Mutton-chop man stared down his nose as he evaluated her in reverse order, from bottom to top. "A fine figure despite her rumpled dress, unbound hair, and"—his eyes widened in surprise, then narrowed in interest when he reached her face—"a wild heritage to augment the setting."

"We're leaving." Brynmor's tone was brisk, but his hand was gentle as he nudged Gus toward the train.

She followed them eagerly.

"If you go, you'll never read..." Ulysses paused to pull a piece of paper, with exactly the right degree of restraint to pique even her curiosity, from the inside pocket of his waist-coat "...this letter from your sister."

Her hopes burst from her throat with a gasp, then came crashing down like a bird blasted from the sky. Indecision froze her in place. The letter couldn't be real. If it were, wouldn't he have mentioned it yesterday in Denver?

"You shameless charlatan," she hissed as he strutted down from the caboose.

Mr. Court ran toward them. "Stay on the train. We don't have time for this."

"Then you should leave, but she will do as I bid when she sees this." He unfolded the paper and held it open for her to read.

The text was in the Cree script and written in Oriole's precise, to the point of fastidious, hand. She leapt toward it. The first line read: *Have gone to look for Wren in—*

He jerked the letter out of her reach and returned it to his waistcoat pocket.

How many hours or days had passed since Oriole had departed on her quest? What if it hadn't gone well? She squelched her panic and demanded, "When and where did you find that letter?"

"Long before you got to Denver's music shop."

His answer was vague enough that she couldn't guess if he was lying.

Brynmor handed Barnum to Gus, then faced her troupe manager with a grim expression. Ulysses' hands twitched. Ready to strike with either his whip or his hidden derringer. She stepped between them. When Brynmor tried to push her behind him, she dug in her heels.

"Predictable." Ulysses' voice oozed contempt. "You leap to shield him, but I know you will soar even higher for your sisters. Sing and I'll let you read all of your sister's heathen code."

"You can't trust him," Brynmor warned.

"I never have."

Ulysses laughed. "You should trust the world even less.

There are worse things than me *out there* wherever your sisters are." The wide sweep of his arm emphasized his words. "And I, at least, want you in adequate condition to perform." As he lowered his hand to his side, his fingers went out of their way to brush his neck.

Her throat convulsed, recalling him choking her while he said, *Do you want me to crush your windpipe? Sing for me, or you'll sing for no one.*

Bailey added bleating to her squirming, seeking comfort or freedom. Neither of which Lark could give at the moment. She needed her hands and mind free to fight. She transferred the lamb into Gus' care as well.

Her thoughts raced through the ways Ulysses could hurt her or hoodwink her. His whip, his gun, his hands, his words. He could've learned a smattering of Cree and forged the letter. Even if it was real, he might not show it to her after she did what he wanted. He might keep demanding more.

None of that mattered. She had to seize every opportunity, even the bad ones, to find her sisters.

When she released a sigh of acceptance, Brynmor did as well. He'd come to know her well.

Ulysses, on the other hand, knew best how to bully. "If you don't sing, trust this. Things will get ugly. People, too." His gaze locked on Brynmor. "Even uglier than they currently are."

Brynmor's smile didn't reach his eyes. "Let's board the train and get this over with."

Ulysses went still. Too still. "Why the hurry?"

"Because," Gus replied as he rocked Barnum and Bailey, who didn't wiggle, not even one little bit, in his arms. "The train has a schedule to keep. Or so I've been told. *Over 'n over.*"

"Schedules must be maintained," Mr. Court said firmly.

Ulysses' gaze remained on Brynmor. "Are you sure there isn't something more?"

Brynmor stood as still as Ulysses. He didn't say a word. Lark's stomach rolled with dread. What plans had he made for his return to Denver? Or for when he was on this train again with Ulysses?

"I'm *sure*," Mutton-chop grumbled, "I'll find *more* whiskey at better prices in Denver."

Ulysses shrugged. "But it won't be Mr. Malone's celebrated brew."

"No, it won't." The elaborately-whiskered railroad chief threw his hands in the air. "I can't believe you acquired every last bottle that man had in stock only moments before I reached his saloon."

Lark had no problem believing it. Ulysses regularly eavesdropped on conversations in order to pounce on opportunities.

"Board the train," Mr. Court urged, "and continue your conversation on your way to Denver."

"My new friends won't be content with what awaits him in that city. Neither will I. Of that I am now certain." Ulysses beckoned to two men peering from behind the caboose's window. "Bring out the whiskey. Why wait to drink and be entertained? It can all be done here."

"No, it can't!" She didn't want Ulysses fouling up this special place. "You can't stay." Her shoulders slumped.

I can't either. If she gained possession of the letter, she'd have a direction. She couldn't linger here waiting for tomorrow's train.

"You shoulda added a bunkhouse before you started yer sheep farm." Gus' gaze went from the lambs to the cabin. "Where do yer visitors sleep?"

"Public accommodations are for the rabble." Mutton-chop puffed out his chest. "My private car has been fitted with the finest furnishings, including a bed fit for a king. This junction holds nothing grand enough to tempt me."

"Temptation," Ulysses murmured, as if the word held the key to everything. "If you heard the right song, you would tell the conductor to roll your railcar onto the side-track, pull the pin, and leave us. All so you could enjoy an evening with my songbird and my whiskey."

Mutton-chop snorted in disbelief. "I don't believe *she* has the power to impress me that much."

"She can, and she will."

The weight of his words made it hard to breathe. The railroad man holding Ulysses' whiskey adjusted his grip on the heavy-looking crate. The cheery clink of the bottles irked her. Ulysses had probably used his last dollar to acquire them. He needed to sell them at a mark-up and quick. His profits always soared when his audience lived in remote locations—like the junction.

Ulysses rubbed his chest, reminding her of the letter in his waistcoat pocket. He wanted her to read it. He needed her to tell him what it said. His odds of that happening increased if she also remained in a remote location—like the junction.

He'd planned this. *All* of this. He wasn't leaving the junction.

"You're safer on the train." Brynmor's quiet words sent the warning bells in her head clanging.

He'd said *you,* not *we.*

Ulysses studied Brynmor closely. "In Denver, you wished to discuss a debt with me." He drawled his next words in the most casual of tones, so the railroad men wouldn't question them. Or guess that, as always, he was manipulating everyone. "Were you hoping to do the same on today's train?"

The cries of the dead rose from their graves. Yesterday's chill dug deep into her bones. Ulysses threw men under trains.

She would not let that happen to Brynmor.

Her plans to keep away from Ulysses wouldn't work. She needed to fall in with his plans, then twist them to her advantage. The first step, same as when she'd let him drag her out of the alley and onto the street in Denver, was to make him believe she was defeated.

She opened her mouth and sang like she'd lost the will to fight, like she'd lost her sisters and Brynmor forever. The fear of that happening hit her harder than Ulysses ever could. Tears burned her eyes. Through them she saw only the junction. Hope strengthened her voice. If she stayed here, she'd obtain a clue to Oriole and Wren's whereabouts. She'd also have a few more hours with Brynmor.

She sang, believing she still had a chance to see everyone she loved. At least one last time.

And Mutton-chop did exactly what Ulysses said he'd do. He told Mr. Court to leave him at the junction. He and his railcar would be staying until the next train for Denver came by.

She made sure no one could change his mind. She kept singing as she led him like the Pied Piper might lead a rat or a child toward her and Brynmor's cabin—the one place where she could find the strength to finish her battle song.

CHAPTER 6

*L*ark's voice lifted Brynmor like an angel's wings and brought him back to their cabin. A place he thought he'd never have the good fortune to share with her again. He held on to Grandpa Gus' arm, so the stubborn old-timer wouldn't veer off track. He made sure his other hand remained free so he could punch the daylights out of Ulysses if he came too close to Lark.

Gus had taken charge of Barnum and Bailey without any protest, but he'd flat-out refused to reboard the train. He kept saying he hadn't seen everything he'd come to see. And now, also hear. The hearing part made Brynmor's guidance unnecessary. At least, so far.

Gus followed Lark as eagerly as the rest of her enraptured audience. Even Caleb looked torn between pausing to listen and leaving to keep his train on schedule. When he handed Brynmor the milk he'd brought for their lambs and trudged off to deal with the bigwig's caboose, he did so slowly and silently.

Only Ulysses acted unaffected. Lark's troupe manager must be tone-deaf. Or so jaded he'd lost the ability to appreciate anything good, let alone extraordinary. He gave all his attention to ensuring the caboose stayed on the sidetrack.

When he finally joined them in the cabin, his gaze took in the tiny interior in one condescending swoop.

Once again, he failed to recognize the extraordinary something that had transformed the room into a highly organized, multi-functional business and home. A rare feat in Brynmor's world.

One only made possible by a true collaboration. As soon as he'd stopped rushing to complete his work and started sharing it with Lark, he'd found his focus.

Lively conversations and experiments about how to use crates to create shelving for freight awaiting pickup, but also everyday living items, had kept them occupied late into the night. A bolt of morning inspiration—or desperation on his part to delay leaving her to go outside to chop wood—had them turning the back of the piano away from the wall to create a divider for a sleeping space in one corner.

A gift for whoever might stay here next.

Not them. Gus needed to go home to Noelle. Lark would be safer there as well. He had to make sure he got them on the Denver to Noelle train when it came through the junction later today. If Ulysses followed them, he'd confront him alone on the train as previously planned.

For now, he must focus on what was happening here—with Lark in their cabin.

Her voice rose as she halted by the stove. She stood where they'd spent the night, side-by-side, together. When her song ended, the silence was shattering.

Until the trio of railroad men broke into applause. "Bravo! Give us another song."

"Give 'er a chance to catch 'er breath," Gus hollered,

then muttered, "Jumpin' Geehosofat, they're demanding." He scanned the room. "Where's my seat for the show?"

Lark joined Brynmor as he escorted the old rascal to the safest seat in the room, a stool behind a waist-high row of boxes.

Gus eyed their creation curiously. "The height 'n shape reminds me of the freight counter at Peregrines' Post."

"That was our inspiration, but we couldn't find a proper countertop." A hoarse undertone ghosted Lark's words. Nothing anywhere near as deep as the rasp that had gripped her voice in Noelle many days ago, but still worrying. Was it because she hadn't sung for a while? Or was she getting ill? Catching a cold or worse?

He grabbed a cup and filled it from the cast-iron jug. Luckily, the water hadn't frozen. He'd have to hurry and build a fire. When he handed the cup to her, she murmured her thanks but avoided his gaze.

"I'll ask my grandsons to help me build a counter for you." The lambs remained wiggle-free as Gus claimed his seat and sat straight and proud as any patriarch.

Brynmor envied his conviction, then drew strength from it. Gus had suffered more than most. He'd survived the War Between the States and the many challenges that followed. A strong heart could carry a person as far as a strong body.

"Thank you, Grandpa," Lark said between sips of water. "Whatever you make will be exactly what we need." Her words weren't a hundred percent true, but close to it.

Gus excelled at woodcarving and leather tooling, but his most recent interest in knitting had produced...*interesting* results.

"Where's yer corral for these young'uns?" Gus' question halted Brynmor's progress toward the stove.

He couldn't ask Gus to hold Barnum and Bailey much

longer, but he also couldn't risk letting two balls of energy roam the room when it held four men who most likely didn't care who they stepped on.

Men who finally stopped gaping at Lark and studied their surroundings.

"Forget about those beasts," one of them ordered. "And that ancient codger too. You should be serving us."

"Yes! Where are *our* chairs?" his comrade demanded.

Their leader puffed out his chest. "We can't possibly stay here. She will continue her show in my railcar."

"I will continue here or no place at all!" Lark gripped her cup so hard her knuckles turned white.

"Gentlemen." Ulysses set his crate of whiskey on top of the piano with a resounding thump. "The bar is open."

While the men clamored for their drinks, Brynmor lowered his voice as he strove to reassure Lark. "If you don't want to sing, you don't have to. We'll find another way to get your sister's letter."

"I'm sorry I brought them here. I should've gone to their railcar, but—" She shuddered. "I couldn't bear the thought of singing *anywhere* but here."

Other than a single violin performance at Noelle's Christmas party, he hadn't heard her do more than hum a song since Cheyenne.

Guilt washed over him for having craved her singing. She'd performed enough to last a lifetime. He shouldn't want that from her as well as so much more. He should be concentrating on doing something that'd help her, like crafting a plan to get her sister's letter.

"There's nothing to apologize for," he said, trying to keep his tone gentle. "We'll find a way to—"

"But I'm ruining our special place!" Her voice grew even huskier, and her eyes glittered with sudden tears.

"You could never do that," he growled. "Even if the walls collapsed and the roof fell, we could rebuild everything *together*." He thrust his fingers deep into her hair and pulled her close enough for their noses to touch. "The only way to ruin anything is for us to lead separate lives."

Her eyes flared wider than he'd ever seen. He'd gone too far, but he couldn't put the brakes on the yearning pounding in his heart. He held on to her and waited for her to push him away. Or, more likely, whack the tender part of his arm like he'd seen her do in Cheyenne when anyone got too close.

Heck, he deserved to be kicked in the groin for touching her this way. She should—

She pressed her lips to his. Shock held him frozen. Then the payload of pent-up emotion he'd bottled up for years burst free. He returned her kiss with love, with adoration and amazement, with the hope that all of his dreams were coming true because this particular one had.

Raucous hooting and poorly played, out-of-tune piano music made them both flinch. Too late he remembered she had an audience. He released her and moved so that the men saw only his back.

Lark fixed her gaze on the few feet of floorboards now separating them. She wrapped her arms around herself as if she were cold and trying to cover herself. Or, more likely, protect herself.

He didn't blame her. He'd behaved like a ruffian, grabbing her and kissing her so roughly.

When Gus stomped his foot, he chastised himself even more. He'd ruined his adoptive grandfather's good opinion of him as well.

Gus wasn't looking at him, however. He scowled at the men across the room. "Those hooligans belong in a pen."

So do I. He'd vowed he'd be different from the lechers who'd wanted a night with Lark. If he couldn't control himself, he wasn't worthy of a lifetime with her.

"That's the answer." Gus' bushy brows soared with inspiration as he surveyed their crates.

"What is?" he asked, glad to hear someone had a solution for something.

"I'll build you a countertop 'n a *gate*. If you added it there"—Gus thrust his chin toward the open end of his enclosure—"you'd have a corral fer yer lambs."

When Brynmor started moving crates to make the gate, or rather a wall, Lark helped him without hesitation. He fought the urge to barricade her inside the temporary enclosure with Gus. If he fenced her in, he'd be as bad as Ulysses.

Her troupe manager kept casting dark glances at them while the railroad men laughed and tormented the piano's keys. One of them paused to yell, "When do we get another song?"

"How 'bout as soon as you tune that piano?" Gus hollered back.

"I should have learned how to do that," Lark whispered. "And repair a violin, too. Then I could've taught Oriole *and* she wouldn't have needed to visit Mrs. Fitzpatrick *and* we might've found each other at a different meeting spot and —" She paused to gulp in air. "And I don't know if I can continue singing without them. Even one song was exhausting."

She'd never been a solo act. Neither had he.

He grabbed her hand. *Idiot. You can't keep doing this. Let go of her.*

Before he could, she clutched his hand in both of hers, like he was a lifeline and she was drowning.

"It's my fault."

He doubted that, but she deserved to be heard, not hushed. "Tell me what happened."

She stared at their clasped hands and spoke in a monotone. "Oriole wanted to escape by train, but I worried Ulysses would telegraph his thugs to intercept us at a station. I insisted we stow away in a hay wagon. When the driver found us, he accused us of attempting to steal his moonshine—hidden in the hay as well. We bolted. I should've sprinted after Wren and trusted Oriole to follow. Instead, I hesitated and lost sight of both of them as they veered down different paths. I failed them, and I'm all they have. If something happens to me, promise you'll—"

"No. Nothing will happen." He couldn't contemplate a world without her somewhere in it. "I *promise* I'll protect you and your sisters." He pitched his voice as low as he could. "Now tell me how I can help you get Oriole's letter?"

"Provide a distraction." Lark spoke as quietly as him, but her voice now resonated with conviction. So did her eyes. She met his gaze head-on. "Like you're doing with me now."

Her ability to rally herself amazed him until he realized this was how she'd survived for so long. She'd learned to keep fighting even if she thought it was hopeless.

"What kind of distraction?"

"A big one, so I can pick Ulysses' pocket."

She'd have to get dangerously close to the man to do that.

His chest grew tight, rejecting that eventuality. "He's too savvy to fall for any sleight of hand."

"He'll fall for anything if he's properly discombobulated." Her voice grew even stronger.

Like him, she found her power in a purpose. They both needed something to reach for.

"Why don't I knock him completely unconscious?" He

frowned at her hand in his. *Why* did every road ahead lead to him having to let go of her?

"His new friends might object."

He heaved a sigh. "We're outnumbered."

"And out of time," Gus muttered. "A storm cloud's rollin' our way."

Ulysses strode across the room. Brynmor released Lark's hand and braced for the bombardment.

The scoundrel stopped with the crates between them. His expression turned haughty as he tried to stare down his nose at Brynmor, like the railroad bigwig had done to Lark. Even though Brynmor's height put him well above Ulysses, the cocky so-and-so did a fine job of making him bristle.

The man had seen the kiss he'd shared with Lark. Judging from the hoots and hollers, the whole room had. What vile comments would they make about a kiss Brynmor had dreamed about for years?

Ulysses' voice dripped with disdain as he said to Lark, "Is your *fragile little* throat rested? I may tell the rabble otherwise, but I know you can't hold an audience for long with your voice. You're not Wren. So, you'd better find an instrument and—"

Gus grabbed a pair of spoons and waved them in Ulysses' face. "Why don't you just hand these to the lady 'n stop flappin' yer gums like some no-talent trout washed up on life's riverbank?"

Ulysses glared at Gus like he wanted to whack the old-timer with his own offering.

Brynmor suddenly wished they hadn't built the corral and Gus was still holding the lambs.

Lark pulled Gus as close to her as the crates would allow. "Playing the spoons is an excellent idea. Their lively tune never fails to turn my shortcomings into Ulysses' windfall."

Ulysses rubbed his hands together as if the money he craved already caressed his fingertips. His voice boomed as he announced Lark's next act. As soon as she started, he slunk around the men, soliciting funds for the continuation of the entertainment. The men told him to shut up and wait. When he kept talking, they hastily forked over their payment.

What else would they pay for? Or become even angrier about paying? Brynmor stoked the stove and waited for his cue.

When Lark finished her song, he announced, "This is my cabin."

It wasn't, but he now deeply wished it were. Lark had called it their special place. He might not be able to hold on to her, but he could buy this cabin and hold on to it for her.

"If you want to stay here and listen to more songs, you'll pay me a fee."

A stunned silence followed his words as everyone gaped at him.

Everyone except Gus. "Charge 'em fer their chairs, too!" he hollered from his corral that now seemed more like a castle on the other side of the room.

That tipped the scales. Or rather, the crates the men had claimed as seats. Roaring with outrage, they swarmed Ulysses. A fine distraction. Except Lark couldn't reach her target.

Luckily, Ulysses didn't stay put. He slipped free of the men and his unwieldy coat. He dropped it without a backward glance. An unholy light glittered in his eyes as he stared at Brynmor and straightened his tailored waistcoat and ruffled shirt sleeves.

The room was too small to go anywhere except out the door. He stood his ground. He wasn't leaving Lark with an unhinged troupe manager and three cranky railroad men who now argued amongst themselves with their backs to everyone else in the room.

A smile curved Ulysses' lips. "Your meddling days are over."

A blur swooshing by their heads made them both duck.

Water doused the shoulders of the railroad man standing closest to them. The man's shriek rose soprano high. The icy spray made Brynmor wince in commiseration.

Lark tossed the now-empty water jug at Ulysses, forcing him to catch it or get hit in the face.

The railroaders spun in search of the water's source.

"Yer bartender did it." Gus thrust his finger at Ulysses. "He's holding the evidence."

"Because she threw it at me." Ulysses raised the jug as if to hurl it back at Lark.

Brynmor slammed him against the nearest wall. "You've finally gone too far." He took great pleasure in using all of his weight to pin all of his opponent, including his arms, against the logs.

The jug hit the floor with a thud.

"Unhand me," Ulysses snarled as he struggled to free himself. When he couldn't, he yelled at the railroaders. "You know it wasn't me. There wasn't time to—"

"Yer fast, but I still saw you," Gus crowed. "Plain as day. Or clear as night. Or both. It was plainly clear."

"But *why* would anyone do this?" The leader of the railroad men demanded, as he gestured to his drenched friend.

"You're in the middle of a family squabble." Lark shoved her palm flat against Brynmor's chest as if to stop him. "And you're getting too close."

Without thinking, he leaned into her touch, eager to savor it. The increasing pressure she applied to his chest made him halt. She was reminding him that he wasn't helping her cause. There was probably more to it, but right now all that mattered was getting the letter.

He swatted her hand away. He didn't get a chance to see if his aim succeeded in directing her toward Ulysses' pocket.

Ulysses lurched forward. The man's forehead missed his chin by a hair, but his knee struck his groin full force. The pain slammed him back on his heels. Too late he understood Lark's words, or rather her warning. Ulysses hadn't survived this long without being a brawler.

"Hit the floor," Ulysses hollered. "He's got a gun!"

The only weapon was the one now in Ulysses' hand. The tiny derringer had finally made an appearance from under his sleeve.

Refusing to give in to the agony gripping his bollocks and crumple to his knees, he fought to stay standing and pin Ulysses' wrist against the wall again.

"Glory be! I've got his weapon." Ulysses' smirk was much too gleeful for his surprised act. "I'll have to shoot him to protect all of *youuu!*" The gun blasted the ceiling in unison with his last word rising as high as the voice of the man who'd been doused in ice water.

"*You,*" Ulysses hissed as he cradled his elbow against his chest and glared over Brynmor's shoulder. "You heathen witch. How dare you keep raising your hand against me?"

"Calm yourself, Uncle. You and your arm will survive even if your pride may not."

Brynmor stole a glance in the direction of Ulysses' still-scowling wrath.

Lark backed toward the door with Ulysses' derringer in her hand. After she'd hit his arm, he'd dropped the gun, and she'd caught it.

His pulse skipped a beat. *Glory be and hallelujah.* She was the most beautiful and resourceful heathen witch to ever grace his world.

"Let us all be happy," Lark said in a quiet but firm tone, "that I've taken control of the weapon you were so concerned about."

"You'll hang if you kill me." Ulysses didn't bother to act as if he were afraid of that outcome. "Then who will protect your sisters?"

Brynmor shoved him harder against the wall. "Stop lying about who's threatening who. She's pointing *your* derringer at *the ceiling* and not you."

Or at least she had been when he'd last looked. What if Ulysses had finally pushed her too far?

A gust of frigid air shot up his spine. A chorus of groans and grumbles rose from the floor where Ulysses had told the railroad men to hide. Behind him, the door—that he hadn't heard open—slammed shut, and the breeze terminated.

"The gun and its last bullet have parted ways in distant snowdrifts," Lark said. "You can release him now."

Did that mean she'd retrieved the letter?

Ulysses' brows arched in a haughty and hard-done-by expression. "You'll both pay for–"

Brynmor kneed him in the groin as he let go and stepped away from the man's foulness. Ulysses slid down the wall and said no more. The sight made the affront to Brynmor's manhood a little less painful. They were even for tonight's abuse but not for the ruin of his eye or every injury Lark and her sisters had suffered at the villain's hands.

Gus cheered and clapped. "I agree that we've all paid enough."

"So do I," Lark said as she went to stand near Gus. "Any more songs that I sing today will be free."

"And I won't charge for the venue or the chairs." Brynmor repositioned himself to remain between her and Ulysses, who either was still incapacitated or playing possum.

"What about the water incident? A free round of whiskey would make for a mighty tasty apology." Gus smacked his lips.

Brynmor found the nearest blanket and handed it to the railroader, whose hands shook as he removed his sodden jacket. "Pour your own drinks. Then gather 'round the stove to warm yourselves while Mr. Stone and the lady rally themselves for the remainder of her performance." His mind scrambled for a way for Lark to read the letter without being observed. He grabbed the sheet music that'd fallen to the floor beside the piano and gave it to her. "Perhaps you will find your next song in these?"

"Thank you." She took the sheets and retreated to the farthest corner, away from everyone, including him.

She had to be eager to finally read Oriole's message. The oversized sheets would conceal that activity from view. If she'd the time to retrieve the letter.

He heaved a sigh. If she hadn't, they'd be in for more clashes, but at least no shootings. Unless Ulysses or their audience had other hidden firearms. He'd never owned a gun. Would he be better able to protect Lark if he had one? Her troupe manager would definitely test his commitment to pulling a trigger.

He couldn't waver. He wouldn't. His black-hearted opponent wouldn't either.

Sooner or later, one of them would have to cast a death blow.

CHAPTER 7

For the second evening, Lark sat on her bedroll beside Brynmor. Together, but no longer alone. Gus slept curled up with Barnum and Bailey on the other side of the cabin. The piano concealed him from view, but did little to muffle his snoring.

They hadn't made the Noelle-bound train. Gus had consumed too much whiskey and wouldn't budge. Brynmor had been keen to carry him and their lambs onboard. Mr. Court had been eager as always to help, but the engineer and boilerman had refused. They were still cross about having to make up for the earlier delay caused by stopping and then offloading the caboose. And why stop at all at a junction that didn't have a working water tower?

Tempers were rising about that failure. Soon the train might not stop here ever again.

Mr. Court had barely had enough time to explain the situation from the train as it slowly rolled through the junction. He'd given them more milk for Barnum and Bailey and promised he'd update Robyn and the Peregrines about Gus' whereabouts. And theirs too.

Outside, on the other side of the tracks, Ulysses and his cohorts continued their drinking in the caboose, where they now played cards. Their distant voices sporadically punctured the junction's moonlit stillness. Complaints outnumbered celebrations, which meant Ulysses was succeeding, as usual, at stacking most of the cards in his favor.

None of that mattered. Not when she and Brynmor had won one gamble and might win more if she bet boldly.

They'd fed the lambs and eaten their own tasty dinner that Brynmor had expertly assembled from the rations left behind by the station attendant. Now they faced the stove, sitting so close their shoulders almost touched as she pointed to each symbol on Oriole's letter and explained what it meant. One day, she might not be able to read a letter to him. She needed him to have every means to help her sisters.

Oriole would not have supported her decision to share their language. Her standoffishness toward the Llewellyns had been as passionate and as unusual as Wren's curiosity. Oriole had not fallen in love and then been shown a new life in Noelle and the junction. She was busy finding her own way.

Lark prayed her sisters were getting help and not hurt, but each time she read Oriole's letter, both her hopes and her worries grew.

Have gone to look for Wren in the rangelands outside Denver. A woman of her small size and legendary quiet was seen with a band of Romani travelers. I might find her with them if you don't find her at the shop.

Meet you, same place and hour, two days later.

Their new meeting day was tomorrow. The timing didn't

leave much room for maneuvering. With Mr. Court's drive to keep his train on schedule and a bit of luck, it'd be enough. And if she could enlist Brynmor's brothers' help, she might stop Ulysses from following her and Brynmor to Mrs. Fitzpatrick's music shop.

She wasn't sure exactly how to stop him. She just knew she must.

After so many days searching, if he finally saw all three of them within his grasp, he'd do everything to hold on to them. Or at least to Oriole and Wren. He'd postulated before that if Lark were gone, his earnings might not be as high, but they'd be more easily gained.

Ulysses' arrogance blinded him to his own vulnerability. She couldn't let Oriole or Wren avenge her death and meet their own at the end of a hangman's noose.

Brynmor gave her a sideways glance as if he'd heard her worries or maybe shared them. "What will he do when he discovers the letter is no longer in his pocket?"

She shrugged. "He'll suspect I took it."

"And then?" Brynmor scowled in the direction of the caboose.

The railcar having its own stove was a godsend. So was Brynmor amassing enough wood to deposit a generous bounty, or barricade depending on your perspective, at the foot of the car's door. The men had warmth and whiskey. They also had money to lose, and Ulysses was busy taking it from them.

No one had a reason to disturb her and Brynmor until morning.

She shifted her seat to face him fully. When he didn't do the same, she said, "We have one more night together."

"And then?" he repeated, as if he couldn't stop thinking about tomorrow.

One night wasn't enough, but it was all they might have. She leaned closer to him. "He'll demand to know what the letter says or follow us and find out."

Brynmor's gaze fell to the letter he still held. "He'll be itching for a fight."

"Don't even think about waging a private battle on tomorrow's train."

"What if that's the only way to—"

"If we aren't going to work together, then why did I bother to show you this letter?" She snatched it from his fingers and threw it into the stove's flames.

Brynmor's gaze finally locked on her, but he didn't turn his body. The line of his shoulders grew even stiffer under his sheepskin coat. Why hadn't he taken it off? Or even unbuttoned it?

"Are you planning on going somewhere?" she asked.

"No. Of course not."

"Then why are you still wearing your coat?"

"I…" He pulled the sheepskin tighter around him. "I may need to bring in more wood."

He didn't need his coat for that. The woodpile was just outside the door, and the stove was so hot that sweat now beaded his brow.

She pressed her fisted hands flat against her knees. She didn't want to fight with him. Especially not in their cabin where they'd shared so much in such a short time. "You're hiding something from me."

"It's not what you think." His frustrated sigh sent a frisson of longing through her body. "You know I always want to be with you—if you're certain that's what *you* want."

"I want you beside me the entire time we're on the train. Can you do that?"

He nodded. "We'll stay together."

"Together, but still apart?" Her hands clenched into fists again. "Why did you return my kiss in full view of our audience, but now that we're alone, you'll barely look at me?"

"We rushed that. I'm not hurrying whatever comes next. I need to know you're sure where this might lead." He removed his coat as he turned to sit facing her and gestured to the tenting on his trousers. "I swore I'd never coerce you in any way."

"And you haven't. But you've tempted me. Many times. So my choice is certain." She abandoned her bedroll. His lap made a much better seat. Warm and welcoming. Hard and hot. Her perfect home. Except for him propping his arms behind himself, still keeping his distance.

She tugged his shirt upward. He raised his arms enough to help her pull it over his head. So much of what she'd admired from afar now lay directly under her fingertips.

His rumbling sigh shook him and her. He fell like a tree. When she went with him and stretched out flat on top of him, his arms finally enveloped her.

A knock rapped on the back door.

"Ignore it," she whispered against his lips. Her words were as much for herself as for him.

His mouth claimed hers, and she couldn't speak. He was done waiting, and so was she. Her hands went to his trousers.

The door latch rattled as someone tried to open it. And failed. Both doors were barred from the inside, and nothing could make her open them.

She had her hands full. She'd found another way to encourage Brynmor to press even closer to her.

The knocking came again. Louder. More determined.

"Leave us alone," Brynmor snarled. "There's nothing for you here."

The voice outside sounded apologetic. "I'm looking for Grandpa Gus."

"Robyn!" They gasped his sister's name as one.

They also scrambled to their feet together and raced toward the door. Brynmor donned his coat on the way. She ran a hasty hand over her dress as he fastened enough buttons to cover himself and flung open the door.

Robyn stood staring at a pair of snowshoes propped in the nearest snowbank. Even in profile and shadows, her pale skin looked rosy from the chill outside or from guessing what had been going on inside.

Despite the cold flooding through the open door, Lark felt her cheeks heat as well. She wasn't one to blush with embarrassment or frustration, but she'd only recently achieved a truce with Robyn. It'd been more than nice to have her as a friend and not a foe.

"Sorry to intrude." Robyn busied herself brushing the snow from her feet. "Especially when you were so generous to give me my own space in Noelle, but I had to—"

Brynmor yanked his sister inside and into a bear hug.

Robyn returned his embrace with equal enthusiasm, then chuckled as her gaze went in the direction of Gus' snoring. "I hoped he'd be here, but I couldn't be sure."

The Llewellyn siblings had always been close, but she'd never seen them hug until this Christmas. Now they embraced every chance they got. Maybe they were making up for lost opportunities.

A lump rose in her throat along with a fierce yearning to wrap her arms around her sisters again. She copied Robyn's recent actions and busied herself. She closed the door, barred it, and also sealed her lips so as not to disturb the reunion.

"What happened?" Brynmor muttered. "Didn't Court tell you where Gus was?"

"I left before the train arrived."

"I should've known. I should've—"

"Relax, *Big Hill*." Robyn's tone was teasing but also deeply admiring as she said her brother's nickname. "You can't do everything."

"I could do more, *Little Red*, if I learned the telegraph. I didn't expect to see you, or rather Max, until the next train from Noelle arrived. How did you get here so fast?"

"I took Birdie's snowshoes and trimmed some time off the hike down the old wagon road."

Lark's jaw dropped as she blurted, "You walked here?"

Robyn was a true trailblazer.

Brynmor held his sister at arm's-length so he could stare at her as well, but not in amazement or admiration. A muscle twitched in his clenched jaw.

Robyn shrugged as if her trek was no big deal. The maneuver got her out of Brynmor's grasp. Or maybe he'd realized it was time to let go again. The return of his frown told her he wouldn't be able to let go of his worries so easily.

"I see you've been busy." Robyn circled the room, pacing more than inspecting their handiwork. "Caradoc had a long day's work as well. So I left him sleeping in his stall and came as the crow flies."

Caradoc was the Peregrines' and Robyn's trusty Clydesdale. Like many workhorses, he was dependable for both riding and hauling freight.

"Rob." Every inch of Brynmor had hardened into the disapproving big brother. "You care for that horse's well-being more than your own. Only the daft or the—"

"*Desperate or the devil travel the wilderness after dusk.*" Robyn finished his sentence without pause or effort.

How often had she been given that warning? Even Lark had overheard it more than once.

"This isn't like what happened to Pa." Robyn raised her palms placatingly. "And I usually agree with your advice, but not this time."

"You could've fallen off a cliff in the dark."

"Have you seen how bright the moonlight is out there?" Robyn folded her arms.

Brynmor mirrored her pose. "Did it reach under the spruce canopy?"

Their disagreement ended in a glaring match. Even the voices in the caboose outside had ceased. The silence—ruffled only by Gus' snoring—made her sigh in relief until she remembered every lull was temporary. How shrill would tomorrow's strife be on the train or at the music shop?

She moved to stand beside Robyn. "Most journeys have challenges, even those during the day."

Robyn shot her a grateful look. "And now I've found a new trail. We have more options for travel and visits."

Brynmor's shoulders sagged as he rubbed a hand across his brow. "Don't tell Gus."

"I won't." Robyn glanced in the direction of Gus' still unbroken snoring. "I'm happy he slept through my arrival. He must've been tired after his adventure."

"You must be too." Lark went to their bedrolls and re-arranged them so there were now three.

Robyn helped her, and so did Brynmor. Their alone time was over.

"After everything that went on this Christmas," he said in a peeved tone, "you'd think everyone would be content to stay close to home until spring."

"I couldn't wait for the next train to find Gus."

If Robyn couldn't wait for trains, then why did she have

to? Why couldn't she blaze a trail straight through the wilderness to reach her sisters? Because she didn't have snowshoes and wasn't dressed like Robyn.

She contemplated Robyn's work clothing with envy and then inspiration.

They were the same size. If she traded her red jacket and striped skirt for Robyn's brown overcoat and trousers, she could travel more quickly *and* less conspicuously. Ulysses wouldn't follow her.

"Don't worry." Robyn took a step back, misinterpreting Lark's intense stare and sudden silence. "I'll take Gus home on the next train to Noelle. Then everyone can stop fretting."

Involving Brynmor and his brothers in her plans was one thing, but putting his sister in the middle of them? He worried the most about Robyn. She did the same with Wren.

She couldn't let Ulysses follow Robyn and suffer his temper when he discovered he'd been duped. She'd search for spare clothing at the Denver office. If she found none of Robyn's, she'd make do with whatever she did find. Even Brynmor's much larger garments might work.

But what about him? How could she disguise him? Other than his brothers, extremely few men matched his size.

They'd promised to stay together. She'd told him she was certain about them. She had to find another way because if she went to the music shop alone, there might be no going anywhere together after that.

A person could only forgive so many betrayals.

CHAPTER 8

*A*t the opposite end of the Denver-bound railcar, the door opened. Without looking in their direction, Ulysses claimed the first empty seat, which put him across the aisle from two lean and hungry-looking men. None of them said a word.

Their silent disinterest agitated Brynmor as much as the busybodies' whispering from two days ago.

Across the aisle from him, Lark was once again tight-lipped. After checking the locomotive and wood car for stowaways, they'd sat with their backs against the wall closest to that car, so no one would sneak up behind them. Directly opposite him and Lark were Gus and Robyn. All four of them sat as close as possible to the aisle and the door behind his right shoulder, where they could barricade themselves if need be.

All of their challenges resided in this passenger car or had to enter it to reach them.

At the end was the caboose with the bigwig and his cronies and Caleb, who was addressing the many complaints they'd made upon rejoining the train. In the middle, a coach with unknown travelers.

The engine's full head of steam rocked their car and everyone on it, but not Lark's gaze. She stared straight at Ulysses.

"Remember what we agreed upon," Brynmor said.

She nodded. "Don't let him get close to you. He still has his whip, and he may have acquired another revolver."

"Together we will defeat him." His sister's smile was confident. Her faith warmed and worried him.

He'd told Robyn everything Ulysses had done. But when he'd asked her to wait at the junction and take Gus on the next train to Noelle, she'd announced her new plan.

"We stay together and fight in pairs." Robyn raised an eyebrow as if daring him to contradict her. "You and Lark. Me and *Bon-papa*."

Brynmor sighed. His sister knew when and where to turn the conversation. Just enough to make him think her way would work. That it might even have been his idea.

"I gotta mean kick," Gus said. "Strong as a mule, I am." He also had his hands full, carrying both Barnum and Bailey. A task he'd insisted upon.

Robyn's hands were free. She'd deliberately and very carefully strapped her snowshoes to her back. Lark's hands were fisted on her lap. The frown on her brow mirrored the one tormenting his.

Changing her mind once it was set would be like trying to roll a boulder up a mountain. Possible. But it'd take a helluva lot of time and effort. The same was true for Robyn and Gus.

Ulysses finally said something to the men beside him. A very brief something that, at this distance, couldn't be heard.

"Do you know them?" he asked Lark.

"No, but he must." Her gaze remained on Ulysses. "Otherwise he'd be talking nonstop, trying to recruit them for one purpose or another."

Something thumped the roof above him. The sound repeated. Like a footstep.

"He's got men climbing over." Lark spun to face the door behind them.

Brynmor jumped into the aisle before she could. The door burst open. A frost-covered man leapt through, brandishing a rope as if to lasso him and—

"Tie him up 'n throw him under the wheels." Ulysses' voice roared down the railcar along with the pounding footsteps of the men who'd help carry out his order. "Then bring me the girl."

No matter what happened to him, he couldn't let them reach Lark or Robyn or Gus.

The rope grazed his head as he ducked. He seized the man's collar and jerked down. Straight toward him as he rose up. His forehead crunched his adversary's nose. Blood flew. So did the man. Backwards out the door. He went with him, charging into him like a ram.

A blur of icy white whipped by on either side. Only ending when they crashed into the woodbox on the other side of the landing linking the cars.

Above the racket of wheels clattering and wind howling, the door banged shut behind him. Lark, Robyn, and Gus had barricaded themselves outside with him. In a precariously small space. Too close to the man he wrestled.

Brynmor wound up to headbutt his opponent again.

A rope flashed over his head. The cord circled his neck, squeezed tight, and yanked him backward. Against his ear, someone's breath puffed, fast and hot as an engine's furnace. Ulysses' men were fighting in pairs as well.

He had to break free before Lark or Robyn joined the fray.

He slammed his elbow repeatedly into his attacker's side. He also staggered like a drunk as his lungs screamed for air. His knees hit metal. Through a wave of starbursts obscuring his view, he groped along the floor for a weapon. His fingertips scratched wood.

He seized the block of timber and swung it over his shoulder like the upward stroke of an axe.

Whatever he hit was solid. The impact reverberated down his arm and up his neck.

The stranglehold loosened. Air returned. He gulped it in. His throat burned, but his vision cleared enough for him to lurch to his feet and spin in search of his adversaries. He found Lark and Robyn—with Gus sandwiched between them still holding Barnum and Bailey—bracing their backs against the door. A wallop on the other side jolted the portal and them.

Ulysses and his men would soon push through. Unless he added his weight to halt them. He stumbled on his first step, shaken by the sway of the speeding train and the now crystal-clear view before him.

Lark aimed a tiny gun at him. Ulysses' derringer. She hadn't thrown it in the snowbank like she'd said. She'd also said, *He'll fall for anything if he's properly discombobulated.*

The word described how he felt. Until he felt something else. Someone's blasted hot breath on his neck again.

"Get down!" Lark yelled.

Once more, his knees jarred the landing. The crack of the gun echoed off the overhang above him while a man fell beside him, howling and clutching his bloody shoulder.

The barrel of Lark's derringer darted sideways to point at his first attacker, identified by his wood-battered face, standing behind him with the rope. The pounding on the portal grew louder. Lark, Robyn, and Gus bounced against it as if it were the saddle of a bucking bronc.

"My finger isn't steady on the trigger. So lie down," Lark snapped. "Before you go down with a bullet."

When her target obeyed, Brynmor took his rope and tied him before he could challenge Lark's bluff. Unless she'd found more ammunition, the double-barrel derringer was empty, having fired its first bullet in the cabin yesterday.

The man she'd shot today didn't get up, but he swore murderous revenge. There wasn't enough rope to bind both men. He'd have to use the strings from his sister's snow-shoes. And hurry.

From inside the car, the next blow struck like a blast of dynamite. The door flew open. The trio, who'd held it as long as they could, flew as well. Gus held on to the lambs. Lark and Robyn held on to him. They made it easy for Brynmor to catch all of them by seizing one thing. Gus' coat.

The arc of the door tossed them sideways. They crashed into the man Lark had shot. He skidded dangerously close to the edge of the landing. So did they.

"Don't let go of Gus," Brynmor yelled to Lark and Robyn as he grabbed the nearest handrail.

The man beside him clenched a groove in the floor. Slick with snow churned up from the wheels, his fingers slipped on the metal. His eyes widened with disbelief, then horror, as he realized his mistake. He flailed his arms. Reaching for the handrail.

Instead, he caught the web of Robyn's snowshoes strapped to her back. In a gut-wrenching whoosh, his weight yanked her over the edge with him. Gone into the white abyss.

"Rob!" Brynmor roared.

A boot kicked his side. The pain turned his anguish into fury. Keeping hold of Gus' coat, he scooped up a block of wood and surged to his feet. Lark rose with him. She kept her derringer pointed at the men while he swung his club. They pressed forward together and pushed the men back into the railcar.

The wall of retreating bodies kept Ulysses from setting one foot on the landing.

"Cowards," he hollered. "She can't shoot you. That's my gun, and it isn't—"

Brynmor slammed the door on his revelation and set all his weight against it. He couldn't move until the train reached Denver. He couldn't leap after Robyn or even look to see where she fell. Despair buckled his legs. Still holding on to Gus, who still held on to their lambs, he sat with his back braced against the door. "I'll never see her again."

"You will." Lark knelt beside him and leaned toward the edge. "I'll be your eyes."

He used his free hand to grab her skirt. "Be careful!"

She strained to peer back along the track.

"Did she—?" His throat constricted, hurting worse than when he was being strangled. He couldn't ask if his sister had gone under the wheels.

"She's lying on the snow beside the track."

She'd been wearing similar colored clothing to the man who'd fallen. "How do you know it's her?"

"It's her hair."

Hair as red as blood. He squeezed his eyes shut, trying to force the thought from his mind.

Lark's hands shook him. Her strength and beauty filled

his vision. Her face may have lost all color, but she didn't shiver from cold or fear. She didn't blink as she stared at him. "I have to go."

His panic doubled. "What else did you see?"

"The man who pulled her off. He's crawling toward her."

"No." He shook his head violently. "He can't—" He sealed his lips and kept shaking his head. "You can't." He couldn't ask Lark to endanger herself to help his sister.

"I have to go because *you have to stay*." She captured his face between her palms and held him still. "Only you can hold this door and keep them from reaching Gus and the engine. Don't let them reverse the train. If they climb over again, pull the pin and split the train in two. Wait till the last moment. Give me distance and time. My best odds are fighting the one man trying to reach Robyn, rather than the many men on this train."

He tugged her skirt, and her, closer to him. "I can't ask you to do this."

She let her forehead rest against his. "You can't stop me either."

"We promised we'd stay together."

Gus spoke for the first time since they'd been forced from the passenger car. "Then we all promised Robyn we'd fight in pairs."

He couldn't breathe. Could only whisper one name. "*Lark*."

"Brynmor. *Mor*." Tears glittered in her eyes. "*My* mor." She hid her face against his chest. "I want to see you again."

"I'll find you." He hugged her tight for a heartbeat, then let go.

If he used his strength to suppress hers, he might protect her in this moment, but never again. She'd never trust being held and still being free.

She didn't move. "Will you meet me at the music shop?"

"I will." *Or die trying.* He sealed his vow with a kiss on her bent head. "We'll gather your sisters and keep them safe with my family in Denver."

"If I were free to go anywhere, my feet would fly back to our time at our junction." She pushed herself away from him and leapt off the train.

CHAPTER 9

*L*ark raced down the street. Her legs and lungs burned, begging her to stop. She sped up. They'd left the deep snow behind. The path beneath their boots had been packed by many wheels, hooves, and feet. Maybe even her sisters'. But not Brynmor's. He and Ulysses would come from a different direction.

The music shop was directly ahead, but the train station was on another edge of Denver. Behind her, Robyn cautioned her to slow down before they fell down.

"Tell me when you can't keep up," Lark called over her shoulder, then cringed with guilt.

Robyn's ability to get up and keep up and also lead the way half of the time was the reason Lark had reached Denver so quickly.

"Just did." The brevity of Brynmor's outspoken sister's reply made Lark stumble.

Robyn had said precious little since she'd regained consciousness from her fall, then stood up as spry as Gus from his, and instructed Lark on how to use the snowshoes. Taking turns with them had allowed them to outrun the man whose heavier body weight sank him deeper in the snow as he chased them. The fact that he kept having to stop to tend to his bullet wound had worked in their favor as well.

They'd lost sight of him around the time they'd reached Denver.

A sudden wave of exhaustion made her halt. Robyn had to be even more shattered from snowshoeing two days in a row. They both needed to rally their strength for whatever happened next.

When Lark wrapped her arm around Robyn, Robyn did the same. They continued side-by-side at a brisk walk, only made possible by going forward together. Their breaths rasped in unison as well, like the ticking of a clock.

She hadn't had time to check her watch. She pulled it out now. If Brynmor's train had kept to its schedule, it would've arrived a while ago. She surveyed the streets surrounding the music shop. She didn't dwell on the alley she'd hidden in two days earlier while hoping to see her sisters.

Brynmor had said he'd find her. If he didn't, she'd find him.

No more waiting. No more if or even when. There was only right now.

And the corner of the music shop was right in front of her. Pressing close to its wall, she crept the last few feet to peek in the window. Mrs. Fitzgerald's commanding tones rose in conversation with a second voice she knew much better.

Her heart leapt with joy. Oriole was inside. The glass distorted her sister's figure, but not the color of her dark-brown hair or the fern-green dress she'd been wearing when Lark last saw her.

"Take it if you want it so much." Oriole shoved something into the shop owner's arms.

Mrs. Fitzgerald's stillness made the object unmistakable. A violin. Oriole's violin. "I need the truth more."

"I can't give that to *anyone*." Oriole's voice broke on a despairing note.

Lark yanked open the door and sprinted to her sister's side. To defend her or console her, she wasn't sure.

Oriole seized her in a hug. "Where have you been?"

"Hunting for you. Didn't you receive the letter I left for you?" Lark glared over her sister's shoulder at Mrs. Fitzgerald.

The woman carefully set the violin on a counter, then ran her hand over her perfectly contained hair. Not a strand had dared to leave its bun. Whatever she felt she needed to compose was inside, not out. "There wasn't time. She just arrived."

Oriole held her at arm's-length and searched the space behind her. "Where's Wren?" When she found only Robyn, her eyes flared wide. Startled and startling.

Lark was reminded how beautiful and different her sister's eyes were. The blue ring circling the amber starburst made a vivid contrast.

"Why is she following you?" Oriole demanded.

Wren may have been intrigued by all of the Llewellyns, but Oriole, as usual, had been suspicious. She'd only been her sweet self when... Lark struggled to remember a time and couldn't. Oriole had *never* been anything but tart around any of the Llewellyns. Why hadn't she recognized it until now?

"Robyn and her brothers are helping me."

"All of them?" Oriole shook her head. "That's impossible."

"You have every right to question us." Robyn's sigh sounded a lot like Brynmor's as she turned to close the door. "But even Heddwyn has promised he'll—"

"We can't stay here." Oriole pulled Lark past Robyn and out of the shop.

"What about your violin?" Her sister leaving it behind was a sight she'd never seen before.

"Forget about it." Oriole's pace quickened as she muttered, "I wish I could." When Robyn and Mrs. Fitzgerald followed them out onto the porch, Oriole swung to face them and snarled, "Keep away from us."

Lark gasped in disbelief. "Oriole, look at them. They're not a threat."

Robyn leaned against the shopfront. Mrs. Fitzgerald's hand rested on Robyn's shoulder, holding her steady. Or maybe it was the other way. The older woman swayed like a tree severed from its roots.

Oriole backed away from them, dragging Lark with her. "Looks can be deceiving." When she stepped off the walkway and out from under the porch, the sunlight made the amber in her eyes flash as orange as the bird her mother had named her after.

The familiar sight made Lark's heart ache. She loved her sister and all of her differences. But Oriole hated being different because it too often drew negative attention her way. The missionaries had called her Devil Eyes. Their audiences had called her worse. She'd been taught to be wary of anyone who stared at her for long. Since a stage performer was constantly looked at, she'd become continually and increasingly suspicious.

"We can't trust them." Oriole kept retreating. "We don't need them."

"What if they can help us find Wren?"

"I nearly found her. All on my own." Oriole raised her chin. "She left before I reached the Roma."

"We'll continue the search together, but first I need to go to the Llewellyns' office. Ulysses attacked us on the train ride here. I must make sure Brynmor's all right."

Oriole dropped Lark's hand. "What happened to getting as far from Ulysses as possible?" She backed away from Lark now as well. "What about gaining our freedom?"

Her stomach rolled as if tossed by a storm. The anchor of her sister had vanished. She tried to catch her hand.

Oriole darted out of reach. "If you're free to stay here, I'm free to leave."

"Wait!" Mrs. Fitzgerald rushed to the edge of the walkway. "I must tell you about your father."

A gunshot cracked. The porch roof above Mrs. Fitzgerald's head splintered. Everyone ducked. Lark grabbed Oriole at the same time Oriole grabbed Lark. Robyn pulled the shop owner back inside as more bullets hit the porch and forced them in the opposite direction.

Lark and Oriole scrambled into the nearest alley and took cover against the wall. Oriole's hand now clasping hers comforted her more than the shelter or the halt of the gunfire. She still had her sister. They peered around the building as one.

"Can't see the shooter," Oriole whispered. "But it's probably Ulysses or one of his men."

"It's him. Unless his railcar didn't make it to Denver." Her heart twisted with dread. What if Brynmor hadn't made it either? What if he was fighting Ulysses far away and with only Gus for help?

"Why would he want to harm Mrs. Fitzgerald?" Oriole asked.

She hadn't a clue. She only knew what she'd seen. "The

shooting started when she made her final plea to stop you from leaving."

"He doesn't want us to stay with her." The breathlessness in Oriole's usually controlled voice increased Lark's bewilderment.

"She mentioned your father."

"She's mistaken," Oriole snapped. "She doesn't know him."

Lark strove to keep her tone calm as if they weren't discussing a world-altering revelation. "She knows something. And we know Ulysses prefers we have no family but him."

Oriole huffed. "He doesn't want to lose his title of uncle."

"His power is crumbling."

An exchange of bullets erupted across the street. The gunman hadn't left. Who was he shooting at now? And who was firing back? If Ulysses was here, then so was—

"Brynmor." She'd never seen him holding a gun. Had he picked one up only to be shot down? "I have to help him."

Oriole yanked her back to her side. "You won't do anyone any good by running into a fight blindly."

Across the street, a man hollered, "Ulysses Stone, this is the sheriff. I saw you shootin' at those women. I gotta take you to jail."

"You can't escape." The unwavering baritone of Brynmor's voice turned her legs to jelly as relief swept through her.

He was here! He was alive and well.

She looked to her sister to share her joy but was met with a frown.

"We've got you boxed in. Throw down your rifle and come out with your hands up." Heddwyn had said more words than his brother, but—as was true to *his* nature—he managed to say them twice as fast.

If Griffin was with them and the sheriff, they'd have the four sides to their box.

In the building directly across from the music shop, a door opened a crack. Then flung wide. Ulysses barreled out, feet flying, arms pumping, one hand grasping a rifle. He sprinted straight for her and Oriole.

From the lanes flanking the building, two nearly identical auburn-haired giants gave chase. Brynmor and Heddwyn gained ground on Ulysses with each stride. She scanned her side of the street. Griffin wasn't there. Ulysses had been wise to challenge the bluff about boxing him in.

A stout man lumbered through the doorway that Ulysses had used. Probably coming from his post covering the back of the building. His voice confirmed his identity as the sheriff when he hollered, "We've got you!"

He should've kept quiet. He should've let Brynmor and Heddwyn catch Ulysses before announcing his victory.

"Look out!" she yelled as Ulysses swung around and raised his rifle.

His first shot kicked up a dusting of snow close to Heddwyn's feet. Brynmor tackled his brother as Ulysses fired again.

She raced toward them. Oriole followed her until Ulysses resumed his charge toward them. Then she yanked Lark sideways, pulling her off the street and onto the walkway.

"Let me go! I have to—"

"Use her shotgun," Oriole ordered as she dragged Lark toward Mrs. Fitzgerald, who was struggling to load the weapon. "You're a better shot than me."

She did as ordered. Ulysses fell a dozen strides from her, clutching his side and not his heart. She'd missed her target.

Oriole removed the gun from her unsteady grasp and aimed it at Ulysses. Her hands trembled as well, but her voice was steady as she said, "Even I should be able to hit some part of him now if he tries to get up. You're needed in the street. Take Robyn to her brothers."

Robyn sat on the walkway, breathing raggedly, eyes wide and wild.

When Lark followed the direction of her gaze, her heart stopped, then started up all wrong. She couldn't move or speak or think.

Brynmor lay sprawled on the ground. Unmoving. A swelling circle of crimson stained his coat. Heddwyn knelt by his side. So did the sheriff.

"Wake up, Lark!" Oriole's command barely penetrated her stupor.

Brynmor was dead. Because of her.

"Change of plans!" Oriole kept shouting. "Mrs. Fitzgerald, *take my sister* to Heddwyn and the sheriff. Help them carry Brynmor into your shop. Hound them every step of the way to hurry. Make sure Robyn gets inside as well, then remind Heddwyn that he's the fastest. He'd better run, quicker than he ever has, for the doctor."

CHAPTER 10

One week later...

*D*espite maintaining a steady pace, when Lark reached the train tracks and altered her course to follow them, her heartbeat sped up. Her destination was in sight.

She'd made it. Every step had been worth it. Except for leaving Oriole.

Ulysses was in jail for crimes witnessed by a lawman whose testimony couldn't be altered by bribes or threats. With this unprecedented situation rendering him unable to control them, they'd agreed to become more self-reliant. They'd each purchased a compass and a pair of snowshoes and expanded their search for Wren.

Then yesterday Oriole had insisted that, to double their chances of finding Wren, they must split up and continue separately.

Her sister planned to roam the rangeland with an old mare and an even more ancient shepherd's wagon that she'd found while looking for Wren at the Romani camp. With just a bunk bed and a stove under an arched-roof box, Oriole's new home on wheels was smaller than the railroaders' caboose.

Oriole wanted nothing more. She spoke only of securing her independence and finding Wren.

But there was so much more. *Like my Mor. And our special place.* Lark had to go back before she could go anywhere else.

She could've taken the train, but Oriole had challenged her to complete the journey on her own steam, without any assistance or restrictions. She'd trekked cross-country to her junction, which now had a station attendant.

The woodpile had been doubled. The pumphouse hummed with life. The train could fill its boiler from the now-functioning water tower. During that regular reason to stop, the attendant could load freight. A stack already waited by the track.

The current freight man excelled at his work, but it was said his assignment was temporary. She'd come to discuss a more permanent arrangement. Judging by the smoke rising from the cabin's chimney, he was inside or nearby. He wouldn't have gone far with the freight sitting outside.

She lost her rhythm with her snowshoes and stumbled. Why was the freight already outside? The train wasn't due for—

When she consulted her watch, her chest constricted with disbelief. The train was scheduled to arrive now. Had it really taken that long to get here? She sprinted toward the cabin door.

Why hadn't she set out earlier? Because her nervous excitement about what might happen today had resulted in a restless night. And, as was frustratingly typical, she'd only fallen asleep shortly before she should have risen.

Not even snowshoeing nonstop had made up for the lost time.

She must hurry before the train arrived and prevented all hope of a private conversation. When she reached the cabin door, she tore off her snowshoes and jammed them in the nearest snowbank. Then she raised her hand to knock on the door.

Before she could, it opened.

Two lambs bounded out. Disbelief followed quickly by elation made her heart race even faster. She thought she'd never see Barnum and Bailey again.

She scooped them up so that the man filling the doorway didn't have to. She didn't want Brynmor to strain the wound that had landed him here, recovering at the least busy office maintained by the Llewellyn and Peregrine families.

The weight of the lambs made her gasp. "They've grown so much in a week!" When she glanced up and finally met Brynmor's gaze, she struggled to breathe at all.

He gazed at her with the hugest smile she'd ever seen. "Our little bounders aren't so little anymore."

She hugged them close, praying she might soon do the same with Brynmor. "No one told me you kept them."

"I asked them not to. I didn't want you worrying about me tending to them. You have too many worries." His smile waned, and a familiar sigh rumbled deep in his chest.

She leaned toward the sound, wanting to be close to everything that was uniquely him. "You shouldn't be exerting yourself." *You nearly died.*

He removed the distance between them with a single step. "Maintaining this junction is the most important work I can do right now." The heat from his body comforted her as well as his words. "I had to ensure our place didn't become a ghost town you'd never be able to find refuge at again."

Appreciation and admiration for everything he did made it impossible not to smile and try to tease a smile from him in return. "Someone told me *our place* is too small to be called a town."

"That someone is elated that you're finally here." His fingertips skimmed her hair as if she were made of glass and might shatter under his touch. Or disappear.

She pressed her cheek into the cradle of his palm. "So am I." Her gaze drank him in like the clearest water.

He looked better than ever. He faced her head-on. He didn't try to hide his injured eye.

"Why didn't you give Barnum and Bailey to Max and your sister?"

"Because *someone told me* the imps adored me. No one needs them as much as I do." His gaze went to her snow-shoes before locking on her again. "Waiting for you to walk out of the wilderness was a lonely business."

The train whistle made them both flinch. When he let go of her, she shivered with loss.

He took the lambs from her, put them back inside the cabin, and closed the door. Then he claimed her hand, and the chill vanished. She held on to him tightly as they walked toward the tracks.

"How much time do you have?" His voice lowered to a grumble. "When must you leave me? Tell me you've heard something good about Wren?"

"I have news about everyone but her. Mrs. Fitzgerald visited the jail and had a long look at Ulysses. She says he's her brother's son."

"Then that would mean..." Brynmor shook his head as if

amazed. "He wasn't lying when he said he was related to Oriole. He's her cousin."

"I've often speculated he added just enough truths to make his lies credible."

"Does Oriole believe Mrs. Fitzgerald now?"

"No, but I do. She showed us her son's inscription inside the violin. Oriole said it could've been added when she brought in the violin for repairs two years ago."

"Mrs. Fitzgerald has a good heart. I hope her wish to have a granddaughter in her life comes true."

Lark hoped for the same. When they halted by the tracks, she leaned against Brynmor and sighed in bliss.

"Are you tired?" he asked. "You must be. When the train arrives—"

"I'm fine." She didn't want to think about leaving his side, but the sound of the locomotive chugging toward them was clear now. "We're making progress. We know Ulysses' reason for shooting at Mrs. Fitzgerald. He lied about being Oriole's only living relative. He wanted to make that lie a reality."

"He'll stand trial for two counts of attempted murder." Brynmor's gaze dropped to her hand in his. "You're finally free. You can go anywhere with your sisters."

"Oriole wants to hunt for Wren on her own." The rising din of the train, as well as the sight of its engine puffing smoke as it rounded the bend, made her rush to say, "I don't. That's why I'm here. To ask if you'll join me."

He grabbed her other hand and held her close as he faced her head-on again. "Lark, if we do this, we should—" He dropped to his knee, then winced as if he'd moved too quickly and disturbed the wound in his chest.

"Be careful. I can't lose you."

"I feel the same. That's why I'm down here. On one knee before you."

One knee? That usually meant— Her thoughts spun with hope. So did the world around her. She really should've stopped to rest at least once on her way here.

A mountain of a man rose in front of her. Brynmor's arms held her steady against his chest. The train's brakes screeched as it prepared to stop.

"I want to spend the rest of my days with you," Brynmor hollered above the clatter. "Here at our junction, or wherever you must go."

"Jumpin' Geehosofat!" The familiar expression came from the train. "Are we too late?"

Lark dreaded the same. Was Grandpa Gus once more leaping off the train before it stopped?

With a package clutched in one arm and his free arm waving wildly at them, Gus stood on the train's first platform —held securely there by Robyn and Max, who shared matching mile-wide grins.

"Have we missed the wedding?" Max ran his hand over his neatly trimmed beard as if puzzled, but his eyes said differently.

Robyn's gaze held the same teasing glint. "Do you need any help, big brother?"

"I *need* a minute. Do not let anyone off that train." He pulled her closer and said her name like a plea, "*Lark*, I fell in love with you in Cheyenne, and I've never stopped loving you. Do you love me?"

"With all of my heart." She flung her arms around his neck.

"Will you marry me?"

"Yes!"

When he whooped and lifted her off her feet, she felt

like a bird soaring heavenward. Wrapped in Brynmor's love, she had no fear of falling.

"Can we get married right away?" she asked. "I'm done waiting."

"I ain't so fond of it either," Gus called from the train. "Can we join you now?"

"Depends. Little Red? Dog Bone?" Brynmor's gaze went from his sister to his brother-in-law. "Tell me you brought a preacher."

"Sorry, Big Hill," Max said with true regret. "Closest one's in Denver."

She sighed in disappointment and then acceptance. The rapid-fire round of their nicknames combined with their easy banter made the delay easier. The Llewellyn and Peregrine families' camaraderie was as uplifting as Brynmor's embrace.

Robyn winked at her. "You'll appreciate this inconvenience later. Hedd and Griff wouldn't give any of us a moment's peace if you two married without them in attendance."

The conductor sprinted toward them, coming from the direction of the water tower where his crew filled the locomotive's boiler.

Lark waved at him, happy to see him in his usual industrious good health. "Mr. Court, we're in a hurry to get to Denver."

"Me too." The young man laughed. "*As always*," he added with a sigh, but didn't stop smiling. "Climb aboard, and I'll fetch your lambs from the cabin, while Max and Robyn load your freight."

"I want to help. What can I do?" Gus leaned toward them, keen to get off the train.

Robyn held him back while waving them forward. "Bryn

and Lark are coming up here, so you don't have to go anywhere, *Bon-papa*. Remember, you need to give them your gift."

When they joined Gus, he proudly presented his package swathed in sturdy burlap. "I carved a weddin' present fer both of you."

His conviction that there'd be a wedding brought a lump to her throat. "You're very wise, Grandpa, to know we'd marry."

"Well, truth be told...I just hoped. A lot. But I know one thing fer sure." He thrust his finger in the air. "Everyone can use my gifts. I make 'em special fer each of you. It's a sign."

"A sign of what?" Brynmor asked with a bewildered chuckle.

"Open it 'n see," Gus urged.

"It's not the right proportions for a countertop," Brynmor whispered in her ear.

That item Gus had mentioned creating for their office would be longer. The plank of wood they held was square.

"Maybe it's the gate," she replied, pitching her voice low as well.

Brynmor kept one arm around her, holding her close as they opened the gift together. It was indeed a sign. A beautifully carved board similar to the one at Noelle's *Peregrines' Post and Freight* office. But this sign said—

"Songbird Junction." The name felt familiar, like a childhood song or a dream. "Where is this place?"

"It's right here." Gus gestured to the track and the cabin, then the earth and sky all around them. "The name came to me the same way you joined us. Swift as a meadowlark arrivin' at an outpost 'n turnin' it into a nest." He tapped the sign. "This is meant to remind you 'n yer sisters where yer needed. Family needs to stick together."

"This is a home for all of us." A rising tide of certainty made her stand taller.

Brynmor's stance mirrored hers. "We'll make sure Songbird Junction lives up to its name. Thank you, Grandpa. Your gift is perfect as always."

"Yes." Lark pulled Gus into her and Brynmor's embrace. "Thank you for being the perfect grandfather."

"Don't forget to give your bride *your gift*." Mr. Court's words claimed their attention. The conductor stood on the landing's steps, struggling to climb up while holding onto Barnum and Bailey and another parcel.

"Caleb." Brynmor hurried to take the parcel. "Thank you for remembering."

"See! I ain't the only one who forgets." Gus' hand on her shoulder stopped her from reaching down to take one of the lambs. He waggled his eyebrows at her. "Never seen a freight man in such a rush to receive a shipment. Must be darned special."

Mr. Court scrambled up and handed Gus the lambs. Max and Robyn arrived and joined them.

"We're all loaded 'n ready to go." Robyn took Gus' sign from her. "You'll need both hands for Bryn's gift."

"Having free hands is a gift in itself." Max pulled Robyn into his arms. When she leaned back against his chest, they both grinned. "Heard Big Hill's gift is more than a handful. Heard he's worried he might want it more than you do. *Heard* we all might benefit from *hearing*—"

Robyn's palm pressed over her husband's mouth halted his teasing. "Shh. Don't give her too many clues."

No one moved to enter the passenger car. They all hovered around her, smiling expectantly.

Except for Brynmor. He held out his gift, wrapped in finely woven cloth, tentatively.

Its shape looked familiar. The weight felt even more familiar. She didn't need to see it—or *hear* it, as Max had joked—to know what it was. "This is from Mrs. Fitzgerald's shop."

"I'll take it back if it doesn't interest you anymore. I don't want you doing anything you no longer want to do."

She pressed his gift close to her chest so she could get as close to Brynmor as possible and stop any further worries he might have with her lips. She kissed him with all of her love. She stopped only to whisper a pledge, "Our home will always have a place for a hurdy-gurdy."

His sigh made her smile. So did his grin, which slanted mischievously along with one quirked eyebrow. "How about a piano that still needs tuning?"

"Until I learn how to complete that task, yes."

"All aboard," Mr. Court called in his most jubilant conductor's voice as he opened the door to the passenger car. "Or rather, all inside. Best take a seat because this train isn't stopping till we reach Denver."

"That's music to my ears." Brynmor reached for her hand at the same time she reached for his. "I'm eager to find a preacher."

"So am I." She pulled him toward the passenger car. "But heading home to Songbird Junction will always be my preferred direction."

She saw her path clearly now. *Find Wren and keep her safe. Make sure Oriole—and everyone who'd become a part of her family—stayed safe. And be happy knowing Brynmor would be safe as well.*

Her hesitation had vanished. Her and Brynmor's clasped hands reminded her that she was strong, and so was he. Their union was unbreakable because they made each other's hearts sing.

Thanks for reading Brynmor and Lark's adventure! If you enjoyed their story, keep reading to see how writing a book review can make an author's day.

And if you're interested in reading Heddwyn and Oriole's story, keep turning the pages until you reach *A Bride for Heddwyn's* excerpt following my Acknowledgments page.

DEAR READER

I hope you enjoyed Brynmor and Lark's journey to build a home for themselves (and hopefully their siblings as well) in Songbird Junction.

If you did, please consider posting a review online or email it to me at Jacqui@JacquiNelson.com

Every single review helps. No matter how long or short, they are a heartfelt gift that is sincerely appreciated. Hearing from readers makes my day and keeps me motivated to write my next book. I look forward to hearing from you!

You can review *A Bride for Brynmor* on Amazon, Goodreads, or BookBub. Or even all three.

AMAZON
amazon.com/author/jacquinelson

GOODREADS
goodreads.com/jacquinelson

BOOKBUB
bookbub.com/authors/jacqui-nelson

STORY INSPIRATION

I have great difficulty speaking different languages, but I've discovered I love the story challenges/complications of including them in my books. I also love the opportunity to link language to a character's past.

- For my Quebec-born heroine (Birdie Bell aka Bernadette Bellamy), I added French in *The Calling Birds*.
- For my American-born heroine (Robyn Llewellyn, whose ancestors came from Monmouth, Wales), I added Welsh in *Robyn: A Christmas Bride*.
- For my Canadian-born Irish-Cree Métis heroines (Lark, Oriole, and Wren, who came from the Qu'Appelle Valley in present-day Saskatchewan), I added Cree syllabics in *A Bride for Brynmor*.

The Métis are specific cultural communities who trace their descent from First Nations (Native American) women and European (first French, then later Scottish, English, and Irish) men who came together during the fur trade in Canada and the United States.

Their unions were often called *marriage à la façon du pays,* which meant "according to the custom of the country." Written with a lowercase m, *métis* is the French word for "mixed."

The Qu'Appelle Valley got its name from a Cree legend about a spirit that traveled up and down the river. The Cree told the fur traders they often heard a voice calling, "*Kâ-têpwêt?*" When the Cree responded to the call, it would echo back.

In French, "*Kâ-têpwêt?*" means "*Qui appelle*?" And in English, that's "Who is calling?" Which is the perfect echo/callback to my story *The Calling Birds*.

Cree syllabics are a script used to write the Cree language. They were first recorded in the 1800s and include nine glyph shapes. Today in Canada, it's estimated that over 70,000 Algonquian-speaking people use the script.

To read more about Cree syllabics and how they inspired my story, visit my website at JacquiNelson.com/the-cree-syllabic

~ Jacqui

ACKNOWLEDGMENTS

Thank you to my *Posse of Book Angels* reader team, my beta readers, and my email list subscribers who not only make my writing journey extra fun but also help make my stories better—including renaming my train conductor who started out as Mr. Smith and then became Mr. Caleb Court.

Special thanks to
Tina Reynolds for choosing Caleb and
Jean Clemens Loftus for choosing Court!

A BRIDE FOR HEDDWYN - EXCERPT
Songbird Junction, Book 2

Secrets are everywhere...

From the moment she met her sisters in a Qu'Appelle Valley orphanage, Oriole has rewritten her past to protect her present. Now Lark is married, Wren is lost, and Oriole is on a mission to find Wren before their cruel and controlling troupe manager does. To succeed, she must cling to her lies and evade the only man she ever let come close, the beguilingly talkative Llewellyn brother who deserted her without a word.

Second chances are few...

From the moment he first heard Oriole sing with her sisters in a Cheyenne saloon, notoriously scatterbrained Heddwyn Llewellyn's desire to change gained focus. Until tragedy struck. To protect his brothers and sister, Heddwyn turned his back on love and the only woman who'd ever riveted his attention—all while refusing to talk to him. Now, after two years apart, Oriole's finally back in his life and so is a shot at redemption.

The Songbird Sisters' quest for freedom may have reunited Oriole and Heddwyn, but it's also tearing them apart. Her sadistic troupe manager is more than happy to maim and murder to get his money-making musicians back. Can two hearts always on the run finally stand still long enough to save each other and their love, too?

CHAPTER I

January 1878
Denver, Colorado

The church bells rang for Lark and her husband, but they'd never ring for Oriole. Unlike her sister, Oriole couldn't depend on love, and no one could depend on her. All she could do was run from her past and present, which included the dangerously distracting Welshman who kept glancing over his shoulder and insisting they needed to talk.

About what he'd yet to say. She wasn't waiting to find out.

Leaving was her best way to save her other sister, Wren.

She must escape the wedding party departing the chapel. In the midst of these six different and not always harmonious voices, her silence grated the loudest. She didn't belong. She was out of tune. Stretched too tight. A strum away from breaking her row in their four-string procession.

First came the newlyweds, followed by the groom's sister and her husband, then the groom's two brothers, and finally her—held in check by the arms of two well-meaning but meddling old-timers. Mrs. Fitzgerald mistakenly believed she was Oriole's grandmother, while Gus Peregrine insisted that everyone call him grandpa whether they were related or not.

Little white lies and full-out falsehoods. They grew like weeds. Around her and inside her. When they'd met at the missionary orphanage, Lark and Wren told her their recently deceased mothers were Cree and their fathers were Irish fur traders they'd never met. She'd yearned for sisters.

Being different made most people shun her, so she'd assigned herself the same history.

One of her first lies in a long list.

A sudden gust kicked up snow in her face. A reminder that today's mild-for-January weather could turn at any time.

"Horsefeathers," Gus muttered as he struggled to keep his beloved flat cap on his head and his ample beard out of his mouth. "Can't wait to move this shindig inside."

When Oriole clutched his elbow to steady him, Mrs. Fitzgerald patted her hand. *She thinks I need help as well.* The grande dame hadn't stopped giving orders since Oriole entered the lady's music shop a week ago, searching for Lark and Wren.

"Our celebration needs a *céilí*. And you, my dearest, must play for us. We're all eager to hear your violin."

"It's not mine." She strove to squash the waver in her voice. She longed to hold the instrument. How could she not? It'd been part of her life for more years than not. "The violin is yours now." *Or at least it is until I find Wren.*

The shop owner shook her head so vigorously her expertly styled—and controlled—cloud of white hair appeared in danger of falling. "Fiddlesticks. You cannot turn your back on your birthright or your talent."

"No one has to do anything if they don't want to." Brynmor's verdict rang loud and clear from the front of the line.

When Lark thanked him, Oriole silently did as well. Her sister was in excellent hands now. For this, Oriole admired Brynmor. And abhorred him too. He hadn't set out to end their tight-knit sisterhood, but he had.

She now had nothing but her quest to find Wren, while Lark had...everything.

Lark held fast to her husband and the gift he'd given her

a few hours ago—Lark's favorite instrument, a hurdy-gurdy. "It's been a long day. All I want is to rest before we catch the train home."

Home. What an odd word. Neither of them had used it except in vague reference to the area where they'd been born, the Qu'Appelle Valley far to the north. Lark and Wren had always spoken fondly of their mothers and their households. So Oriole had done the same. Another lie.

Lark's new home was Songbird Junction, a tiny train stop on the line to the mountain mining town of Noelle—where the couple who walked behind Lark and Brynmor lived.

"I'm keen to get home too." Max Peregrine kissed the crown of his wife's curly red hair.

"And back to work," Robyn teased with an easy smile that shone the brightest for her husband. "You never stop."

"That's because I get to spend my days working with my wife and my nights—"

Robyn's laughter and her palm pressed over Max's mouth cut him off. They'd wed on Christmas Day and now ran the Noelle freight office. An equal partnership made possible because after the Llewellyn siblings' parents died, the three brothers had raised their sister to work with them as wagon drivers.

Heddwyn and Griffin completed the line, walking behind Robyn and in front of Oriole.

"Livin' so far apart is foolish," Griffin snapped. "I'm only toleratin' it 'cause it might help us find Wren."

Although Griffin was the youngest of the Llewellyn brothers, he was also the biggest and the only one with a temper that he struggled to control. She hoped Wren never had to go near him because her tiny sister would be terrified of a gruff giant like Griffin.

"Lark and I will search the area around Songbird Junction," Brynmor said.

Robyn nodded. "Max and I will do the same in Noelle."

"Best get a move on then," Heddwyn added in a rush. "And get where we all need goin'."

Despite the conversation, everyone continued to behave in a maddeningly laid-back manner, except for the man who'd had the last word.

Heddwyn Llewellyn. The charming but scatterbrained brother, whose mesmerizing blue eyes she strove to avoid. He could never keep out of other people's business or stay still. He kept running his hands over his closely cropped auburn hair or his clean-shaven jaw—every time he glanced at her, the damsel in distress.

The charity-case he'd only recently promised Lark he'd help. When they'd met two years ago in Cheyenne, he'd watched Oriole for different reasons.

Fickle man. You have a soul even less dependable than mine.

Last week, she'd been embarrassingly surly with Lark, who deserved only sweetness. She had to leave before she cracked completely. She stopped tracking Heddwyn from the corner of her eye and focused on what lay ahead.

No one else did. Griffin scowled at the ground, lost in his own turmoil. The couples now conversed privately. Even Mrs. Fitzgerald and Gus had struck up a conversation around her, like she wasn't even there, like she'd already gone.

The Denver freight office was close now. As soon as they reached it, she'd find an excuse to run to her wagon parked in the alley behind Mrs. Fitzgerald's Music Emporium. Then she'd drive out alone in search of Wren. And never see Heddwyn Llewellyn again.

The thought made her yearn to look at him one last

time. Another reason to put distance between them. *He doesn't care about you. He has no idea who you are. He's never had the fortitude to look deeper and find out.*

She snuck a peek at him.

The flare of his wickedly gorgeous grin made her cheeks burn as he said, "I've always wanted to say your eyes are—"

"Stop staring," she hissed, then stiffened at her foolishness. When she'd said the same on their last day together in Cheyenne, they'd quarreled.

One of their remarkably few conversations. He was charming with everyone but her.

"I hate being stared at," she muttered as she struggled to keep her own gaze off him and on what lay ahead—the freight office where they'd part ways.

Above the last building between her and the Llewellyns' office, a charcoal cloud rose along with a crackling sound. Her gaze shot back to Heddwyn.

"Turn around," she urged, "and *look* at the fire ahead of us."

He spun in a blur and sprinted away even faster. Gus and Mrs. Fitzgerald's arms around hers prevented her from following.

Loss, then fear, stabbed her heart. "Be careful!"

To read more about *A Bride for Heddwyn*, visit
JacquiNelson.com

If you haven't already, don't forget to add *A Bride for Heddwyn* to your "want to read" shelf on Goodreads at
Goodreads.com/jacquinelson

SONGBIRD JUNCTION SERIES

The Llewellyn Brothers
Western Historical Romance Trilogy

Welcome to SONGBIRD JUNCTION, where Welsh meets West in Colorado, 1878. The journey to find a forever home and more starts here...

Brynmor, Heddwyn, and Griffin Llewellyn are three Welsh brothers bound by blood and a passion for hauling freight —in Denver, where hard work pays.

Lark, Oriole, and Wren are three Irish-Cree Métis sisters-of-the-heart bound by choice and a talent for singing—in any place that pays.

Will the frontier train stop of Songbird Junction be their families' salvation? Or their downfall when the sisters' troupe manager—a con artist who calls himself their uncle but cherishes only his own fame and fortune—demands a debt no one can pay?

Claim your ticket to travel from America's booming small-towns to the most promising train junction in the Rocky Mountains' snowbound wilderness where—during three perilous quests for freedom, truth, and harmony—the final destination will always be true love.

FREEDOM. TRUTH. HARMONY.

Bride for Brynmor - Book 1
Can a sister who's lived only for others find
freedom with one man?

A Bride for Heddwyn - Book 2
Can a sister who's lied to everyone find
truth with the wrong man?

A Bride for Griffin - Book 3
Can a sister who's lost her voice find
harmony with the right man?

PRAISE FOR THE NOELLE, CHRISTMAS STORIES...

The Calling Birds
Noelle, Colorado - Christmas 1876

"Jack and Birdie's story is suspenseful, romantic, sweet story of family, trust, love and survival. I couldn't put this story down!" ~ Carter and Conners Mom

"With secrets, outlaws, greed, and love this all provides for an amazing adventure." ~ Sandra S.

"An unforgettable read. Lovable characters, page turning plot, and satisfying resolution to all kinds of conflicts." ~ Deutsche OMA

"Birdie is a delight sassy woman who knows how to stand her ground...I loved the humor, the fear, the race against time" ~ Cyn

Robyn: A Christmas Bride
Noelle, Colorado - Christmas 1877

"The perfect book to set the mood for the Christmas spirit!" ~ Maria D.

"Beautiful story of friendship, love, and forever happy ever after." ~ Tonya L.

"I loved this book. It was revisiting old friends" ~ TJW

"Jacqui has hit a home run with this one!" ~ Peggy C.

THE CALLING BIRDS - EXCERPT
The Fourth Day in the
Twelve Days of Christmas Mail-Order Brides series

A wanted woman's flight,
a man in pursuit of honesty, not stolen gold...
and only nine days left to save the town.

Many years have passed since **Bernadette Bellamy** fled the
Cariboo Gold Rush and her reputation as the sister of a
French-Canadian gang of thieves. Armed with only an
honest talent for sewing and a willingness to lead a solitary
life on the run, she stays one step ahead of everyone seeking
her brothers' last—and now lost—heist. Until a craving to
settle down makes her reinvent herself as **Birdie Bell**, a
dress shop owner. The arrival of an old foe combined with
her desire to hold onto her treasure trove of fabrics has
Birdie joining a wagonload of brides bound for a remote
town.

After losing his leg and his wife, **Jack Peregrine** buries his
pain under a mountain-high pile of work. He only agrees to
sign up for a mail-order bride to save the town of Noelle,
keep his freighting business, and care for his absentminded
grandfather. But Jack's request for a sturdy bride who won't
crumble under his burdens brings him a woman as tiny as
she is troubled. Can two mismatched people band together
to become the perfect match?

THE CALLING BIRDS

Noelle, Colorado
December 24, 1876

A crowd of women filled *La Maison's* front hall. One of them was Jack's bride, Birdie Bell. A hard-working woman who'd started her own dressmaking business in Denver. A mature woman of thirty. A strong woman who wouldn't break under life's hardships.

Maybe his luck would change today. With time Miss Bell might come to respect or maybe even enjoy his company. He needed this marriage to last.

He should've looked for his grandfather first, but he couldn't stop his gaze from scanning the women in search of his bride. Even wild-swept from the storm and huddled together shivering from the cold, the women were a fine-looking bunch. How had Mrs. Walters managed that?

A raven-haired, pale-skinned woman standing slightly apart from the rest snared his attention. Her beauty would've been enough to hold any man spellbound, but her tiny size turned him rigid with concern. A woman so small wouldn't last long in a town like Noelle.

His worry turned to anger. Whoever had asked her to come here should be horsewhipped!

A faint smile curved her mouth, as if she was amused by the prospect of being housed in a location as scandalous as La Maison. He must be dreaming. She shouldn't be here, and she couldn't be amused.

She surveyed the room, studying everything and everyone—until she saw him. Then she stared at him the way he felt he must be staring at her, as if mesmerized.

"I've come for a bride," a voice proclaimed loudly, a familiar voice that made him cringe. "Which one of you is the future Mrs. Peregrine?"

The woman spun to face the speaker—his Grandpa Gus.

A wave of gasps and tittering laughter swept through the crowd. Several of the women glanced at the tiny woman who'd captivated him. She was now staring at Gus with wide eyes.

Her gaze darted to him. When she caught him still staring at her, her expression turned blank and devoid of emotion. She straightened her shoulders, strode straight up to Gus, and said in a lyrical voice with a seductively foreign accent, "I am the bride you seek, Mr. Peregrine. My name is Birdie Bell."

A surge of euphoria followed quickly by alarm made him stagger and lean heavily against the nearest wall. This tiny Frenchwoman couldn't be Miss Bell. He'd asked for a strong woman. This one wouldn't be able to hold up under his workload, the rough town, or the surrounding wilderness. She'd abandon Noelle and him.

Could he blame her if she did?

If she didn't, she might die here.

"No!" His voice shot out louder than Gus' a moment ago.

Complete silence descended around him. The chance to make a good impression was long gone. Everyone in the front hall stared at him, including his tiny bride.

To read more about *The Calling Birds*, visit JacquiNelson.com

If you haven't already, don't forget to add *The Calling Birds* to your "want to read" shelf on Goodreads at
Goodreads.com/jacquinelson

ROBYN: A CHRISTMAS BRIDE - EXCERPT

The sequel to *The Calling Birds*.
Read what happens one year later in Noelle 1877…

Who's the perfect match for a flame-haired Welsh tomboy who loves driving wagons?

Raised by three free-spirited older brothers, **Robyn Llewellyn** has learned to fight for what she wants—and now she wants to transform her boss and best friend, Max Peregrine, into a lifelong partner. Determined to become the image of what a marriage-minded man wants, Robyn trades her trousers for a dress and heads to Max's hometown of Noelle, Colorado. But changing who she is with the help of the now happily married Brides of Noelle puts her friendship with Max at risk.

Who's the perfect match for a work-addicted Denver business owner who loves his independence?

Defying his brother and grandpa's wishes for him to stay with them in Noelle, **Max Peregrine** has created his dream job—leading a highly successful branch of Peregrines' Post and Freight while working beside Robyn, the only person who makes him smile every day. But when she leaves without a word, Max follows her to Noelle, where the choices they both must face could make it impossible for them to stay together beyond Christmas Day.

Inspired by *My Fair Lady, The Gift of the Magi,* and the spirit of gift giving, *Robyn: A Christmas Bride* is a classic Western historical love story set in a small town high in the mountains during Christmas 1877.

∾

CHAPTER 1

Denver, Colorado
December 21, 1877

"She's gone?" Max Peregrine shouted, disbelief then panic raising his voice to a roar. "Where?"

Lined up shoulder to shoulder inside the Denver office of Peregrines' Post and Freight, the three Llewellyn brothers studied him intently, not with surprise but curiosity. And something more. Something his careening thoughts couldn't identify.

Brynmor, the eldest by several years, heaved a sympathetic-sounding sigh. "She's—"

"Fine," Heddwyn interrupted, embracing his status as the swift-talking middle brother who needed to do everything quick, including driving freight wagons at breakneck speed. He shot his brothers a secretive glance. "Remember our plan. He sounds upset, but we need to know more."

"Stuff your plans!" Max threw down his pencil and stormed around the desk where he'd been working on his ledgers. He'd throttle his answers from Robyn's brothers if need be. "Why—did—she—leave!?"

Griffin, the youngest but also the largest, folded his arms over his barrel of a chest. "He sounds more than upset."

"Good." Standing on either side of their flame-haired baby brother, Brynmor and Heddwyn spoke and nodded in unison, like matching musclebound bookends with the same auburn hair and sky-blue eyes. Except Bryn had one eye clouded white. Max had yet to learn why.

The Llewellyns were fond of talk but notoriously unforthcoming on certain subjects. Like, at the moment, Robyn's departure.

"He's regretting something," Griffin added.

Max froze. Leave it to Griff to pinpoint Max's state of mind while never addressing his own. Griff's hair color matched his sister's, but his reputation as the Llewellyn sibling with a short fuse was his alone.

"I regret"—he unlocked his clenched jaw and tried to speak normally—"that your sister might have put herself in jeopardy."

Heddwyn snorted. "Little Red can take care of herself."

"Hedd's right. The wee one is all grown-up," Bryn proclaimed with another sigh.

"She's as tough as she is beautiful." Griff's gaze narrowed, studying him even more keenly. "Or do you believe otherwise?"

"I don't," Max muttered, thinking of Robyn's lean strength, steely blue gaze, and stunning smile. A smile he'd been blessed to see every day since he moved to Denver. A smile he craved more than a miner coveted gold. A smile that had become increasingly melancholy of late. "Whatever's wrong and wherever she's gone, she needn't be alone. I would've traveled with her."

"You sure 'bout that?" Hedd released a low whistle as he pointed at Max's face. "Look! Dog Bone's turning the same shade of red as Ruddy does when he's near to exploding."

In Welsh, *Griff* meant *ruddy,* but that hothead remained poker-faced as he said, "We have eyes, Peaceful. No need telling us something we can plainly see."

Max's entire body burned with outrage. Not because of the teasing titles the Llewellyns loved to dole out, for themselves and others. In Welsh, *Heddwyn* meant *blessed peace*, a constant source of ribbing for a man who had too much energy to stand still. Max had learned to look below the surface of their name tomfoolery after Robyn revealed her brothers called him Dog Bone because he never stopped gnawing problems into submission.

He didn't give up. A trait all of the Llewellyns found admirable. If they assigned you a name, even one you didn't find flattering, it meant you'd earned their respect. They didn't waste their time on people they didn't like.

Robyn's explanation along with her easy smile had ended his dislike for long conversations. But only with her. They'd talked about everything after that, argued as much as they'd agreed, but always ended up smiling.

No topic had been taboo, or so he thought. Why hadn't she spoken to him before she left? And how could her brothers question his resolve, especially when it came to Robyn?

Their lack of faith left him not only furious but frustrated and flummoxed. "If your sister asked, I'd have gone *anywhere* with her."

Bryn raised an eyebrow in challenge. "You said differently in the past."

"I did not."

"Did too," Hedd shot back. "Then Rob said she had to go there. No other place would do."

"Took the Clydesdale." Griff thrust his thumb over his shoulder. "In better weather, she'd be there by now."

Max's gaze leapt in the direction he'd indicated, hoping to see Robyn behind her brothers. That this was all some colossal joke.

Driven by a fickle wind, his world spun faster than the snow outside the window. She couldn't be gone. Not in such a storm. Not when he needed her, when they all needed her. She was the thread that held everything together. Did her brothers seriously believe he wouldn't have accompanied her on any journey? They'd lost their minds. He couldn't do the same. He had to find Robyn.

To read more about *Robyn: A Christmas Bride*, visit
JacquiNelson.com

Hope you'll add *Robyn: A Christmas Bride* to
your "want to read" shelf on Goodreads at
Goodreads.com/jacquinelson

WANT A FREE E-BOOK?

Deadwood, Dakota Territory 1876...
In a gold rush storm, can an unlikely pair rescue each other?
Raven wants to save one person. Charlie wants to save the
world. Their warring nations thrust them together but duty
pulled them apart—until their paths crossed again in
Deadwood for a fight for love.

EXCERPT
RESCUING RAVEN - CHAPTER 1

Fighting a growing impatience fueled by rage, Charlie
Jennings drew his revolver and urged his horse through the
trees flanking the Deadwood Trail. Below him, an
Appaloosa with the strikingly similar color of his own horse
—white covered from head to hock in chestnut spots—was
rein-tied to the back of a buckboard. If the horse hadn't
caught his attention, he might not have given the transport a
second look.

He might not have seen her.

The wagon rattled forward carrying one silent and seven
grumbling passengers. When a bend in the trail cast the sun
in the eyes of the guards, one riding behind and the other in
front, he charged his spotted mare down onto the road.

Everyone in the wagon, except for the cowering raven-
haired woman, screamed. The driver jerked on the reins.

The horses skidded to a halt. The guards scrambled for their weapons.

The click of his revolver being cocked made them all freeze.

The silence that followed was as heated as the summer sun on his back. The guards glared at him through squinted eyes. He kept his focus on them as well—lined up in a neat row down the barrel of his Colt Peacemaker.

"Jennings," growled the closest man, who went by the name Big Bill. "You shouldn't be here."

"Yeah," hollered Bill's partner, a stranger who resembled a beanpole.

Frontier trails and towns had a way of attracting similarly named men, including the Charlies like him. They also had a fondness for embellishment. The deck was stacked in favor of the rear guard being called Skinny Sam or Loudmouth Pete.

"We heard you were guidin' a miner 'n his four kids, the ones who lost their ma, away from Deadwood." At least Skinny hadn't heard, and used, the double-barreled moniker Charlie had been saddled with since arriving in the Black Hills.

"But you," he shot back, "didn't hear that my job finished ahead of schedule."

"Well," Bill said on a long breath, "ain't that a spot of bad luck."

"Not for one of your passengers." He didn't look her way. He'd already seen enough: a ragtag assortment of women, one hunched with her dark head over her wrists tied to the wagon.

To read the rest of *Rescuing Raven*, visit my website JacquiNelson.com and sign up for my newsletter.

ALSO BY JACQUI NELSON

ABOUT THE AUTHOR

Fall in love with a new Old West... where the men are steadfast and the women are adventurous. You'll find Wild West scouts, spies, cardsharps, wilderness guides, and trick-riding superstars in my stories. Those are my heroines. Wait till you meet my heroes!

My love for historical romance adventures with grit and passion came from watching Western movies while growing up on a cattle farm in northern Canada. I've been nominated for over 20 awards and won the RWA® Golden Heart® & the Laramie® — but my best reward is hearing from readers who have enjoyed my stories.

Email me at Jacqui@JacquiNelson.com

For updates on giveaways, special events, and more, join my newsletter at JacquiNelson.com

amazon.com/Jacqui-Nelson/e/B00EE6GE88

goodreads.com/JacquiNelson

bookbub.com/authors/jacqui-nelson

facebook.com/JacquiNelsonAuthor

instagram.com/jacquinelsonauthor

pinterest.com/JacquiAuthor

x.com/Jacqui_Nelson

youtube.com/@jacquinelsonauthor

tiktok.com/@jacquinelsonauthor